Last Chance for Paris

Last Chance for Paris

by
Sylvia McNicoll

Fitzhenry & Whiteside

Published in Canada by Fitzhenry & Whiteside,
195 Allstate Parkway, Markham, Ontario L3R 4T8

Published in the United States by Fitzhenry & Whiteside,
311 Washington Street, Brighton, Massachusetts 02135

www.fitzhenry.ca   godwit@fitzhenry.ca

10 9 8 7 6 5 4 3 2 1

Library and Archives Canada Cataloguing in Publication
McNicoll, Sylvia, 1954-
Last chance for Paris / Sylvia McNicoll.
ISBN 978-1-55455-061-6
1. Dogs–Juvenile fiction. I. Title.
PS8575.N52L38 2008   jC813'.54   C2007-904596-0

**U.S. Publisher Cataloging-in-Publication Data
(Library of Congress Standards)**

McNicoll, Sylvia.
Last chance for Paris / Sylvia McNicoll.
[240] p. :   cm.
ISBN-13: 978-1-55455-061-6 (pbk.)
Summary: When forced to spend the summer with her twin brother and
their glaciologist father in the mountainous region of Last Chance Pass,
Zanna takes in an injured puppy she names Paris. But when
her brother goes missing, what had begun as a boring and rustic
inconvenience turns into a matter of life and death.

1. Dogs - Juvenile fiction. 2. Family life - Juvenile fiction.   I. Title.
[Fic]   dc22   PZ8.M2385La 2008

Canada Council   Conseil des Arts   ONTARIO ARTS COUNCIL
for the Arts   du Canada   CONSEIL DES ARTS DE L'ONTARIO

Fitzhenry & Whiteside acknowledges with thanks the Canada Council
for the Arts, and the Ontario Arts Council for their support of our
publishing program. We acknowledge the financial support of the
Government of Canada through the Book Publishing Industry
Development Program (BPIDP) for our publishing activities.

Design by Wycliffe Smith Design Inc.

Printed in Canada

For Sputnik, my fellow traveler for thirteen years.
Special thanks to Dr. Richard M. Petrone.
Also to Natalie Anne Comeau, dog trainer extraordinaire.

CHAPTER 1

Hey Zane,

Mom's trying to destroy me. I know I shared the womb with Martin once, and complained when they separated us four years ago, but cooping me up for a week in a pickup truck with him was her perfect revenge. He's the poster boy for emissions control, and you should have heard Dad and him when we were driving through the oil fields. The first rig fueled the longest babblefest ever on alternative energy sources and greenhouse gas effects, blah, blah. They're always trying to educate me! It's been a rough ride crammed in together with them, the few earthly possessions I've been allowed, and all Dad's tools. Up, down, around, and that's just my stomach when they talk. "Look, there's the new Ford hybrid!" I told them just to get them to breathe for a minute. It's like I don't exist to them otherwise. No Internet café in any of the towns where we've stopped. Dad wouldn't let me use his satellite phone. Finally, when we arrived here at the Park Information Office in Last Chance Pass, there were two computers, one marked Out of Order and the other a too-slow chug-along. The connection is dial-up! Really. Last Chance Pass: our destination, the final frontier. Whose last chance anyway? "Only for one summer," Mom says. Which might as well be forever for the two of us. I'm fourteen: I should have a say in my life! Still, don't worry: I won't let her break us up. The park attendant's rushing me: someone is waiting, arrr. Who knew there were other people in this burg? Have to go. Martin is reaching for the keyboard. Love, Zanna

I press *Send* a second before Martin can, then I swat his hand away from the keyboard.

"Ouch. C'mon! Don't you want to see our new home?" My wholesome brother towers over me. He's grown a lot since we last lived together: too much fresh air and sunshine.

"Not *my* home—my summer chalet!" I roll my eyes at Mr. Happy Face. Grinning, beaming brown eyes that look tiny in his smile creases, face round as a glow ball—he looks exactly like Dad. Why not; he's lived with him for the last four years. Isn't that

what happens? We're not identical twins, obviously—
I'm a girl—but I don't even think we look alike.

I'm the brooding type. Learned it from Mom.
Bony face, big dark eyes, and hair to match, if I let
it. Instead, I streak it a bright yellow, kind of a tiger
effect, so that people will stop saying we look alike.
They still do anyways. Moody Mom, moody Zanna.
Dad's already told me a dozen times on this trip how
much I remind him of her. I'm just not one of those
people who smiles all the time without a reason, and
right now, I'm searching hard for a reason to smile
at all. I follow Martin out of the backwoods office to
the truck where my father has packed even more of
the backseat with groceries.

Outside, I breathe in the thin air. The panorama
of iced mountains looks postcard pretty, but the
houses across the street spoil the foreground, the
trim and window frames blistering with old paint,
the yards overgrown with weeds. The sidewalks
buckle and crack in places. There's a "used-to-be"
feeling to the place.

An old lady inches by, gripping a walker marked
with a jaunty maple-leaf flag. She's openly staring at
the ATV sitting in the back of our truck. It looks like
a cross between a Hummer and a tractor: yellow,
flattened-down roof, high cabin, and large treads.
And yeah, Dad and Martin have already discussed

replacing it with a more fuel-efficient model.

"We're filming the next James Bond movie," Martin explains brightly, nodding toward the strange vehicle. "We're the first of the film crew."

I elbow him hard, as her eyes open larger into watery-gray camera lenses and her mouth opens too. I'm about to tell her the truth but she doesn't say anything. Is she not from this country? Or is it not the custom to speak in Last Chance? Instead, I find myself playing along with Martin. We're a team again. I like it. It's my first reason to really smile, and I do. "Yes, and I'm the actress they hired as the new Pussy Galore." Still no reaction.

Martin loses interest in her and scrambles into the front seat. "Shotgun!"

"So immature," I answer, climbing back onto the hard jump seat beside the supplies. He's only seven minutes younger, but since he's a guy you have to multiply that by seven years, I think. I'm still smiling though, because I've missed all his stupidity over the last few years.

My father turns and grins. "Not long now."

Wincing, I fold my arms across my chest as we drive out of Last Chance. I count the streets, and there's maybe ten, max, all lined with more old clap-board cottages. At the town limit, two larger-than-life grizzly bears stand on their hind legs, massive brown wooden paws clawing at the air. Wilderness art. They look like the newest structures in the tiny burg.

We're beyond nowhere, I think as I watch iron-gray rock structures and scruffy green fir trees whiz by. As we turn, a bag of canned goods tips over and spills tinned Spam onto my lap. I push it back in, shuddering. I try never to be that close to dead flesh, canned or not.

"Look, quick! That's an eagle!" Dad jabs the windshield at the top.

The large, winged speck circles, and the truck wobbles. "Watch the road, Dad!" I call, even as I keep staring at the bird. It swoops lower; I can see its white head and black body clearly. Suddenly it dips out of sight, like a story we'll never read the ending to, and we continue to drive. I turn around to hunt for it through the back window, but it's no use. I sigh. Boy, if I could fly, I'd be outta here too.

I don't even *want* to reach the end of our journey; I'm so scared of where I'll be stuck this summer. I've seen pictures of the places Dad lives in when he's in the Arctic. Maybe it will be a cabin with no electricity, running water, or even dial-up. That won't bother my father and brother. They'll like that: "We're reducing global warming single-handedly," Dad will say. Then he'll thump the wall with his fist and explain how the logs are prepared and put together.

"Cool!" Martin will say when he spots the outhouse. "No showers or baths all summer!" And neither will care about communication with the outside world. They have each other: what do they care? Of course, somewhere, holed up in a quaint little flat with a view of the Eiffel Tower, Mom will be sending *I Love You* and *Wish You Were Here* messages through to last.chance@rangerland.ca. My stomach clenches into a fist.

"Check out the waterfall!" Martin calls out.

At the base of a mountain, water crashes into a cloudy white stream bubbling alongside the road.

"Rock flour." My father answers an unasked question. He's a geomorphologist—a fancy name for a guy who studies rocks and glaciers; most people call him a glaciologist—and he can't help sharing. "See the dusty color? Fine particles of stone cause it."

Looks unnatural, I think, like a witch's brew. To me, all the scenery has a sinister, rough look to it. Slate- and pewter-colored stones shoot up on all sides; they feel like fortress walls. So desolate. We veer around another dark bend. "How much further?" I ask, thinking we'll never be able to get to town on our own. No malls, no theaters, no arcades—just fresh air and nothing else. I shake my head.

"Not long now," Dad answers.

"That's what you said three hours ago." Martin takes the words right out of my mind, not even my mouth. It's an uncanny ability he still seems to have, even after our years apart.

"Well, it's all relative, isn't it? Three hours is nothing compared to two weeks, right?" Dad ruffles Martin's hair and Martin grins. I sigh. All their camaraderie makes me feel lonely for Mom, which is strange because we haven't even been able to agree on toothpaste flavor lately.

The truck turns onto a dirt road surrounded by huge, tall cedars, its wheels straddling the grass and weeds in the middle of the track. We bump, bump, bump around and then finally, we shudder to a stop.

My mouth and heart open wide as the sky. This is it. Three similar-looking Heidi houses perch in a clearing. "That one's ours!" Dad points to the first and largest one. With a red shingle roof and honey-colored log walls, the cabin blinks at the world through three tiny red-shuttered windows. I inhale deeply and the fist in my stomach unclenches. A lake in front of the houses sparkles with diamonds of sunlight. The rest of the lake is that unbelievable shade of aqua you see in those postcards of Greece that show the sea, except in spots where it mirrors the silver-capped mountains. I can't help smiling again. It's awesome.

"Glacier silt in the water reflects back the light," Dad explains. "The iron oxides make it that color."

Mediterranean blue, I think, a spectacular shade spoiled by too much scientific knowledge. What's Dad going to talk about in fifty years if all the glaciers melt away by then? I squint at the lake as I breathe out. My heart actually aches. Where's the tour bus, the T-shirt stand, the crowd of tourists with cameras, my mom? She'd love this scenery. I sigh. There's something terrible about a beauty this big and wide and lonely.

"Wow! Look!" My brother points. A large brown creature with a huge rack of antlers on its head stoops, lapping at the water. Is it real? It looks exactly like the stuffed one on display at the Park Information Office. The elk hears or smells my brother, lifts its head full of branches, and swings around toward us, slow and cowlike. Molasses-brown eyes don't blink, and there are no rat-quick city nerves; he stoops again to finish his drink. To the side of me, I hear Dad's camera click.

Golden body and chocolate-dipped head. The elk strolls through the diamond water, barely making a ripple. I have the urge to jump at it, to make it run, kind of the same way my brother tapped on the lizard's glass back at the Park Office to get some kind of reaction from within. I can't take the elk's slow, nothing-happening pace. Something has to happen. Someone has to free me from this slow-mo dream. The elk lifts its head again, ambles up the shore, and walks into the trees.

Click! "Let's check out the house!" My brother switches channels like a remote control. He stomps up the staircase that leads to the balcony and the front wall, that's really just one large window over-looking the lake. Martin jiggles the handle of the sliding door, noisy and loud, shattering the silence, cracking open the tranquil-nature mood.

Still under the spell of nature, I follow more slowly.

"Just a minute, I've got the keys here." Dad climbs up after him and fumbles through his collec-tion. He slips the right key into the slot, twists, and we're in.

"Cool," Martin says.

I just stare. Like the elk in the lake, it's not what I expected.

There's a kind of fake colonial theme running through the cabin. Sparkling new, with a stone fire-place in the corner, a maple-colored log interior, and bright red couches lining the walls, the house opens up at the top into a loft and, in another corner, a galley kitchen. I walk toward it. It only takes about eight steps to cross the cabin. Microwave, built-in stove, oven, fridge—and there are two more doors to the left, off the smallish passageway: a bedroom with a double bed and a bathroom.

What a relief! There's a tub, shower, toilet, and sink. No outhouse usage necessary this summer, even if it does conserve water.

I open a closet door and a curtain rod falls down, barely missing my head. There's a stack of fabric in it, purple with red and blue poppies—drapery of some sort.

Dad picks up the rod and shoves it back into the closet. "Probably left over from the cabin's model-home days." He looks at the poppies on the curtain. "No accounting for taste."

"I like them," I tell him as I move to shut the door.

"Zanna likes something? Really? Let me see." My brother pushes in and stares at the curtains. "Yeah, I can see why." Insincere tone. He touches my fore-head as if to feel for a temperature. Then kicks the door shut. "Come on. Let's check out our bedroom!"

"Excuse me? *Our* bedroom?" Back when we were ten we had bunk beds, and I loved it. Martin always kept my nightmares in check, kidding me out of them: "Did the monster look like this?" He'd cross his eyes and hang out his tongue, and he'd give me tricks for avoiding them. "Never face the wall if you want to have good dreams." But we're fourteen now, and the nightmares I have are totally different.

I follow Martin around the corner. He climbs the steep stairs to the loft, and I scramble up behind him. "It really is only one room. You weren't joking." The room stretches across half the house, bigger than any other. At either end are identical beds, bureaus, desks, and cupboards, bland hotel-lodge-type furniture. A small window doesn't quite light up the room from the center back wall, and of course, nowhere is there a dividing privacy wall. No privacy from my brother's half or the living area down below. "Dad, I can't share a room with Martin. No offence, bro. A girl's got to have some privacy!"

Dad pokes his head into the loft area. "You're not sharing a room, Zanna. Think of it as a backwoods adventure pad. This is as good as it gets!"

Martin and Dad chuckle while I crouch and paw frantically at the baseboard behind the desk for a telephone jack. Nowhere, nothing. "How do we get Internet out here? Do we have broadband?" I look back at Dad.

He shakes his head. "You can go to the Park Information Office anytime you want."

"No, no I can't." I stand again. "Have you noticed how far away it is? It's not like I have a driver's license or even a set of Rollerblades. Or do we have horses?" I ask hopefully, parting the window's red curtains to look around the property. No barn anywhere. I sink down onto a bed.

"Just think how fit you'll get from all that hiking. You won't miss your gym membership at all."

"Yeah, but will I still be able to have cybersex with multiple partners on a public computer?"

Dad's eyes bug out and his mouth drops open. Him and his stupid jokes; that'll teach him. Martin sees the look on his face and falls onto the bed laughing. It's a deep throaty chortle, and I can't help laughing too. "Gotcha!" It feels great to know we still share the same sense of humor.

But then Martin's laughter sputters out and he switches channels again.

"I'm starved!" he says.

"Let's unpack," Dad answers. "Then we can have lunch." They stomp down the stairs without even glancing back to see whether I'm coming.

I ignore them and fling myself back onto the bed, staring up at the wood-beamed ceiling. I'm not even hungry; why should I help? Still, at the thought of food my stomach rumbles to life. Unbelieving, I sit up, touch it, and feel the complaints. After a week of traveling together, surely Dad remembers that I'm vegetarian, doesn't he?

The front door slides open and closed again and again as they empty the car. At least I can miss that joy. I hear the fridge clinking as they stock it with bottles, the cupboard doors banging, bags rattling.

I hear the *click-click* of a manual can opener—how old-fashioned—and, not for the first time, stare down at the strawberry on my left ankle that started this whole ordeal.

A tiny, discreet tattoo; even my grandmother had advised my mother to "Pick your battles and don't fuss over the small stuff."

The scab is healing nicely, despite my mother's warnings about infections and brain diseases that dirt on the needle or lead in the ink might cause.

The strawberry that broke the camel's back, that's what Mom called it. "You're supposed to be eighteen to get a tattoo! How did you talk your way around that?"

"I borrowed Imelda's ID." Imelda is my boyfriend's sister, of course, and Mom hates Zane, my boyfriend, anyway.

Me, I fell in love when I first heard his name, starting with a zee just like mine. "My mother called me that because she was 'inZane' to have me at her age," he'd explained to me.

"Ha! My parents named me Zanna because, after thirty-six hours of labor, my mother yelled 'HoZanna' when I finally came out." We were psychically linked, something Mom obviously couldn't understand since she'd thought nothing of separating me from my twin brother so long ago.

"Zane has absolute control over her," I overheard my mother tell my father on the phone. "You take her this summer. I've had enough." But sending me to Last Chance Pass had nothing to do with Zane, if you think about it. All she had to do was take me to Paris and I wouldn't have seen him again. What kind of mother gives up and throws away her children, anyway? One at a time: first Martin and then me. I yank my sock up over the offending fruit.

The smell of something cooking wafts up. Delicious. I inhale deeply and my stomach growls again. They don't care that I didn't help unpack, they don't care that I'm not joining them. They're a practiced team, those two. What's the use? I head down the stairs again.

"There's meat in this stew," I complain as I lift the lid from the pot.

"You can pick it out," Martin suggests from the bar stool on the other side of the counter. "The gravy only has artificial beef flavorings, trust me. I checked."

"Did you buy any hummus?" I ask Dad, sitting beside him. He shakes his head. I open the bread box in the cupboard. "Could you not find any whole-grain bread?" I stare at the thick white Italian loaf.

"Any tofu?"

"'Fraid not. I did pick up a surprise for you. Third cupboard from the left."

I fling open the doors and pick up a jar of something that looks like...

"Pea butter," Dad tells me. "It tastes, smells, and looks exactly like peanut butter. A Canadian invention for people who have allergies."

"But Dad, Zanna doesn't have allergies, she's just vegetarian."

"Peas are vegetables," Dad answers.

I open the jar and squint at the contents. From down below, I hear a whimper. My stomach shocks me with its new tones of protest. I grab a knife and saw off a couple of thick slices of bread. Then I spread the pea butter on one of them and pat the other slice on top.

I bite into my sandwich and savor the close-to-peanut-butter-taste. A whimper, a growl, a snarl, a yip, and a yowl. It's not coming from me this time. I touch my stomach just in case and feel no vibrations at all. More whimpers. I look at my brother.

He shakes his head and shrugs his shoulders. Dad jumps down from his kitchen stool. "There's an animal under this house."

Chapter 2

MY BROTHER SHOOTS OUT THE DOOR. BY THE TIME I CATCH UP, he's shimmying, belly in the dirt, under some cracked boards in the closed-in area under the balcony.

"Dad, Dad! It's a dog and he's hurt." Only Martin's legs hang out from under the boards.

"Careful!" Dad warns. "What if it has rabies? Injured animals bite!"

Aouuw! As if in protest, the animal howls, long and mournful.

"What should I do then, Dad? He's stuck but he's struggling and making it worse."

"Put your jacket over his head and pull him out." A few moments pass and we hear low growling.

My brother's legs shimmy backwards till his hips appear again. The dog yips and yaps, the sounds more muffled now. Then Martin stops. "Dad, I'm stuck!"

Dad leaps to his assistance, cracking back the wood above Martin's hips. Martin pulls out slowly. The dog struggles in his arms, his head tossing underneath Martin's jacket. Martin takes it off and the animal pants, looking almost happy.

"Why, he's just an overgrown puppy," Dad says.

I squint at it sideways. What a weird-looking creature. A husky pup? He has black and brown markings on most of his body, and a white mask forms the top of a heart around his strange yellow eyes. They seem catlike with curiosity, and fierce. But then his oversize paws and donkey ears give him a puppy-dog awkwardness. His legs dangle over my brother's arms, long and bony just like Martin's.

"We better bandage up that cut," Dad says, gesturing to the red gash on the pup's left front leg.

"Bring him into the house."

As we head to the steps, I notice a padlock on the door cut into the honey-colored boards beneath the balcony. "Look, we could have walked in to get him."

"So that's what this last one is for." Dad holds up the smallest key on his chain. "We'll have to check it out. Maybe we'll find more tools."

A motor scooter would be good, I think, watching him hesitate.

"Dad, let's go!" Martin calls, and we follow him into the house.

In the bathroom, the puppy struggles to get away. I watch from the hall. "Hold his head under your arm, away from me." When Dad dabs antiseptic on the cut, the pup yelps, high-pitched, in pain. Dad wraps some gauze around the wound and tapes it in place. "Make sure he doesn't chew at that. You can set him down now."

The overgrown puppy makes a successful break for it as Martin lowers him. We head into the living area to see what he's up to. He lopes around the small space, yapping at us and stopping every once in a while to sniff and duck away. Something spooks him and he leaps onto a couch, knocking over a moose-shaped table lamp. The ceramic antlers shatter on the floor.

"Heel, sit, stop!" Dad calls, setting the lamp back upright. The moose head now appears to be female. The puppy jumps down and attacks my sneaker.

"Ouch, get off!" His teeth sink through.

"What should we call him?" Martin asks.

I gather up ceramic antler bits from the floor. "We can't possibly keep him!" I shake my foot free of the puppy again. "Look, he's made holes in my Paluzzis already." I stomp my foot. "Shoo!"

"C'mon, Zanna, we always wanted a dog."

"When we were little, sure." I remember begging in stereo, Martin on one side and me on the other, when the tenants' dog next door had puppies. Me: "Please, Mom, we'll walk him." Martin: "We'll feed him." Both of us: "We'll never ask for anything else for as long as we live."

Mom said no. "The apartment is too small. We travel too much. Dogs are too much work." A long list of "too's," all of which still apply.

The puppy growls, yellow eyes still hypnotized by my Paluzzis, ears up antennae-style. "Besides, he must belong to somebody."

"What do you think, Dad?" Martin asks.

Dad shakes his head. "He's big, but he's young. No collar or tag. It seems more likely some dog had a litter out here and left this guy behind."

I think of Mom again, probably sipping a cappuccino in a little café right next door to the Eiffel Tower. "Paris," I sigh.

They turn to look at me: Dad, Martin, and the oversize puppy.

I didn't mean to say that out loud and I don't want them to know I was thinking about Mom, who would never let us keep an animal. "We should call him Paris."

At that moment, the puppy jumps toward my sneakers again.

"It's like he already knows his name," Martin says.

"He sure does love Zanna." Dad smiles. "Paris it is."

"He loves my designer sneakers, is what he does." I throw up my hands. "Look at this place. It's too small for this animal. Besides, we have to at least try to find his owner," I sputter.

"That's right," Dad agrees. "If we find an owner, Paris has to go back." He's using that special tone, just humoring me. He doesn't think Paris has an owner.

Martin and the dog grin. So does Dad. I'm the odd woman out. Even the husky puppy is very obviously a male. A sinking feeling inside tells me the sneaker-chewer is here to stay.

"We should go back to town and check with the animal-shelter people. There may be someone looking for him right now." That way I can also see if Zane's e-mailed me back yet.

"What animal shelter?" Dad frowns. "Why don't you clear up the dishes and give Paris the lunch leftovers, Zanna? Martin, let's go check out the tools under the house."

Floppy paws once again grab hold of my sneaker, claws dig in. "Hey, why do I get stuck in the kitchen?" I shake my leg to loosen Paris's teeth from my shoe. He yips, encouraged by the game.

"We did all the unpacking," Martin answers, and the two of them troop out the door.

"How would you like to have a Canadian invention to eat?" I ask Paris.

The puppy glances up from chewing my lace, head tilting, ears and eyes sharpening.

"Do you want the most yummy-tasting sandwich

in the world? Huh? Do you, boy?"

The puppy's tail is wagging like crazy now, moving his whole butt from side to side.

"Then let's go." Paris chases after my heels into the kitchen. I rip off a piece of my pea butter sandwich and throw it to him. He catches it in his mouth, and in an instant something on his face changes. His grin drops at the same time as he hacks and spits out the bit of bread.

"Well, that's all I get to eat around here." I finish my slice. He's slumped down on the floor, yellow eyes not blinking at me.

That can't be all, they say.

"Hey, I'm not the one who should be feeding you anyway. Otherwise you'll have to settle for bean sprouts or tofu. No way am I touching meat."

Paris lets out a disappointed yowl. His eyes beg for something else.

"Okay, fine. This one time." I grab the pot of stew from the stove and slam it down on the floor for him.

Paris glances up, mouth opening into his favorite toothy smile. Then, in about ten seconds flat, he scoffs it all up. I give him a bowl of water and listen to happy lapping sounds. Suddenly, Paris stops drinking and growls as he races for the door. I hear pounding across the porch and head into the living room. Dad and Martin fill up the vista at the front.

They're carrying a wooden pole between them.

"Martin saw this under the porch," Dad tells me as they continue through the house and up the ladder to the loft. "And he had a great idea."

"Goody," I answer, not understanding the grand find. I step into the living area to watch from the ground. Martin holds the pole, while Dad marks off something with a pencil. Then he begins drilling. Beside me, Paris leans his head back and howls.

"We need to go dog-food shopping," I shout at Dad. As good a reason as any to head back into town and check my e-mail. I'm craving my Internet fix.

The drilling stops for a second. "Give us half an hour here, Zanna. Why don't you go outside with the dog? Oh, by the way, on my bed there's a present from your mother. She wanted you to open it when we got here."

The drilling and howling start again. I grab Paris and haul him up. Whoa, he's a heavy pup. "We don't want a stupid present from the stupid woman who doesn't want us, do we?" I scratch roughly between his ears and Paris scrunches his eyes closed in agreement. Still, after a moment I can't pretend I'm not interested. Nobody's looking anyway, and the bedroom is only a few steps away.

There it sits. A large, brown-wrapped parcel. The puppy jumps on the bed to sniff it. "No, Paris. Food's not Mom's style." I lift it. Heavy. What could Mom possibly think she could buy to make up for all this? Paris jumps down and sniffs at a corner, lifting his leg. "No! Bad puppy!" I scoop him again and rush him out the front door, down the steps. Will he be okay by himself? "Don't go anywhere!" I tell Paris and run back to get the brown package.

Thing is, Mom buys great guilt presents. The Paluzzi sneakers were from when she took off for New York, leaving me at home with chicken pox and *her* mother. I got a cell phone when she missed my grade eight graduation ceremony. When I got rushed to the hospital for an emergency appendectomy (after she told me to go to school, that I'd feel better later), she bought me a new CD player that flashed colored lights to the beat of the music. All of which, sneakers excepting, I left behind in order to travel to Last Chance. This present had better be good to make up for that. When I get back outside, I sit on a rocking chair and rip open the parcel.

It's wooden, a piece of spindly furniture of some sort. I pull open a small drawer and find tubes of paint. I understand. It's an easel. Under the tubes of paint is a piece of paper. Instructions on how to make it stand up? No, it's a note with a picture of a Monet painting at the top. I clench my teeth together tightly as I read my mother's words.

Zanna. You don't believe me now but sometimes it takes a change of place for a person to see her life differently. You and I are so much alike. I think we both need another space right now. I hope you can make sense of your new world with these paints. I look forward to seeing what you come up with next time we meet. Love, Mom

I stare at the painting. It's one Mom and I saw at the Art Gallery of Ontario, in Toronto, together. Soft, purple boats sailing against fiery orange skies with gentle pinks and purple stripes. I read the tiny print to recall the name. *Sunset on the Seine.*

I'm angry with Mom all over again. She's looking at a scene like this right now. I'll bet she sees her life differently all right, surrounded by hundreds of years of culture. Here I am, stuck in the middle of the wilderness. I stare out at the lake, which has changed to a steely color. The mountains skulk in the background, charcoaling the sky; the peaks smolder in a pale mist. My world looks as angry as I feel. Where am I supposed to even get canvas if I do decide to paint? I pitch the easel to the porch and stand up in time to see Paris leap at something.

"Paris, what are you after?"

A huge grasshopper jumps away from his paws and Paris pounces again. When the grasshopper springs, Paris makes a lucky snap for it with his muzzle.

"Ew, let it go!" I tell him but he's already happily chewing. I dash to grab his muzzle but he runs away.

"Come and check it out!" Dad suddenly yells from the balcony at the front.

I give up on Paris and head up the steps. As I slide back the big glass door, I see what Martin and Dad have been working on. The purple curtain with blue and red poppies divides the loft in two. They've mounted it on the pole they dug out from under the porch.

"We can get something different when we go into town for more supplies," Dad says. "But the concept, do you like it?"

My brother grins from his side of the poppies; this is his big idea, after all.

Not exactly a *Sunset on the Seine*. Still, the clashing colors lend the first touch of sincerity to the cabin. "I like it, Dad. Poppies and all. But we have to go into town right now. The dog is so hungry he's eating bugs."

Chapter 3

THE SKY CHANGES QUICKLY IN LAST CHANCE. BY THE TIME we're back in town again, the mountains have no tops anymore, only smoke clouds. Without the alpine backdrop, the town appears even more dingy and desolate, the grizzly sculptures at the gate like fossilized animals instead of art. With a dark brown log exterior and the traditional brown-and-yellow signage, the Park Information Office looks like a frontier fort guarding the other two shops in the strip mall.

"Let's hit the hardware store first," Dad suggests as he sets the hand brake in the truck. Martin agrees. The hardware store and the grocery shop are the other two buildings in the strip.

Paris scrambles on top of me to be the first one out. He'd been the first in the car too, and still wears the yellow rope looped around his neck from when Dad tried to haul him out.

"I want to check my e-mail. You guys go ahead," I tell them.

"Great," Martin says, but then the two of them take off, leaving me with the dog. Can I leave him behind? He may rough up the insides of the truck, but who would ever notice?

By the time I climb out, though, Paris has squeezed around me and, stubbornly resisting the pull of the rope, lands on the sidewalk. "Fine. Just behave," I warn him as we push through the Park Office door.

It's a dark, wood-paneled room with bare antlers hanging over the entrance. To the left is a counter with a couple of desks behind it. The two uniformed guys sitting at them don't really pay that much attention to me until a large, gray muzzled black Lab lifts himself from the younger guy's feet and woofs at us. The Lab didn't bark at us when we were here getting directions. In fact, I thought he might have been stuffed or made out of wood, like everything else around here.

I make sure Paris stays to my right so the Lab doesn't see him.

"Shh, Quincy, just a city girl." The ranger looks about Zane's age. Taller though; broader shoulders, deeper voice. The Lab collapses back down into a heap.

Hey, what does he mean, "just a city girl"? "Hi, I'm going to use the Internet, if it's okay?" I call. The guy waves me on.

Paris enjoys sniffing along the baseboard, slowing

down the walk to the computers, which sit on a center aisle of desks at the back. The whole right wall is a glassed-in display of stuffed wild animals, and by "stuffed" I mean the dead, glassy-eyed ones, not the fluffy toy filled-with-only-new-white-material kind. A black bear stands frozen on her hind legs alongside her cub. A beaver has his orange teeth locked on a branch for eternity. A small field mouse sits stiffly in the earth and an elk, just like the one in our lake, stoops to get a drink that will last forever. Caught in mid-snarl, a wolf wrinkles up his muzzle to bare some pretty scary teeth. Looks like he's eyeing the cute little bunny, also frozen in time, behind a bush. Not much difference between that wolf and somebody's dog—maybe the wolf's a bit bigger and broader across the chest, although Paris is pretty big that way too.

On either side of the center aisle of desks stand a couple of large tanks, one holding a few rock bass and the other, a couple of lizards. That's the glass Martin tapped on last time, and got in trouble for it.

I spot the sign. *Ten-minute limit on the Internet.*

"Hurry up, Paris. I've got e-mail to write." I pull him away from a corner mid-sniff and quickly sit down at the computer, hoping to max out the time and maybe sneak in some more. Paris paces at the end of his rope, though, and the *click-click* of his nails sounds loud against the quiet of the room. Beep, beep, beep, beep! Luckily, the super-slow dial-up sounds even louder. An eternity later, I navigate to a mailer and download my mail. I scroll down, scanning the list: four notes from Mom, subject headers: *Love You, Paris News, Exciting News,* and *Answer Quickly.* I don't click on them. No notes from my Zane. I type in his e-mail address. Then I start my message.

> *Zane! I love you, I love you, I miss you.*
> *You won't believe it, but the Internet connection*
> *here is sooo bad. The mailer here must be*
> *rejecting the notes you're sending me and*
> *there's a Mountie-type coming toward me.*

I type as fast as I can but the younger ranger seems to be heading my way with some kind of purpose.

He's one of those dark, good-looking types who thinks that he can boss everyone around, I can tell. I'm sure glad Zane's not like that. Maybe because he's not handsome in a regular kind of way. I close my eyes and see his face. He has a narrow nose and pale eyes, the same light-gray as a computer screen. His dark hair is chunked with red sections, and it hangs over one eye. He never tells me what to do. He doesn't talk a lot, and he's so laid back that he annoys Mom, which is kind of what I like about him.

This Park guy's staring at me with eyes that are an unnatural blue. Has he got glacier silt for brains or something? I try to ignore him. What's his problem, anyway? "Excuse me, Miss," he says.

"Hey, listen, can you cut me some slack? It took so long to get this connection. And there's no one waiting for the computer." I keep typing. I write Zane all about finding a puppy under the house. How strange he looks, how big and floppy he is. I can smell the ranger now. He's like a pine forest growing beside me.

"You can keep working on the Internet, but you can't bring a wild animal in here."

I look up again. Mr. Good Looks points to Paris at my feet, quietly chewing at my laces. "They're my shoes he's destroying. He's not bothering anyone else," I answer. "You've got a black Lab at the front there."

"A retired rescue dog, sure. He belongs to my dad and he's saved fourteen people."

"Paris is young. Give him a chance. He's already caught a grasshopper."

The guy laughs at me, a deep, rumbling noise.

I miss your laugh, Zane, I type.

"You can't bring a wolf in here," the ranger dude says.

I blink at him. "What wolf? We found this guy

under the house. He's very friendly. He wouldn't hurt anyone. Designer footwear and grasshoppers, maybe. Paris is really just a puppy."

"He's got to have some wolf in him. Look at his eyes, and the way his tail droops. Besides, he's huge. Check out those paws."

"Excuse me, but I don't have time to examine the dog right now. I only have ten minutes on the Internet. And I'm expecting a very important message!" I go back to typing. *I hate a know-it-all*, I type.

This Mountie guy says Paris is a wolf. What would a wolf cub be doing under our house? Sure, he's oversized for a pup and has weird eyes. They do look wild. Did he chase something underneath the house? Why did his mom just give up on him then?

The Park guy coughs. "Listen, my father's going to come over here in a second."

I type like lightning now.

Why don't you write me a snail-mail letter, if your e-mails keep bouncing? My address is RR 32, Last Chance Pass, Alberta. Gotta go, Zane. My ten minutes are really up. Love, Zanna.

I press *Send* and wait a couple of moments to download again in case I just missed him or his address doesn't work anymore. Nothing. What is wrong with this stupid computer? I stand up.

"Did you get your important message?" the Park guy asks.

"No. I can't believe I'm stuck in such a nowhere-land that my e-mails don't even get to me."

"I get e-mails from the other posts all the time. It works fine. Now, can you take the wolf outside?" the guy asks.

"Fine, sure. And my invisible dragon. Paris, come on, we're not wanted." I head out the door, dragging Paris behind me with the yellow rope. Outside, I sit on the bench in front, waiting for Martin and Dad. Paris curls around my sneakers. He's so big I'm reminded of that stupid old joke about a guy's really fat wife. *When she sat around the house, she* really *sat around the house.* Paris's body completely surrounds me.

Across the street, the headless mountains still smoke and the old lady with the walker comes out of the dilapidated house and stares at us. Paris stares back.

"Are you the new people Skylon moved into one of their houses?" The ranger dude suddenly sits down beside me.

"Shouldn't you be in there timing your customers?"

"Taking my break. I'm Tyler Benson, by the way." He stretches out a hand toward me and Paris jumps up, yapping and wagging.

"Shh, Paris." I hesitate, staring at his hand. This guy has been nothing but rules and regulations, but his hand looks friendly, open and reaching as it is. "I'm Zanna, Zanna Segal-Day." He holds my hand tightly and his grip is warm and strong.

"So did you move into one of the Skylon cabins?"

"We're in one of the log huts by the lake, but my dad doesn't work for Skylon. He's a glaciologist on an independent study. You know, documenting glacier retreat?"

"Independent, eh? Betcha he'll find a way to conclude that a ski resort won't harm natural resources in Last Chance."

I stare Tyler down and then I sniff. "A ski resort here? We can only hope." I shake my head. "Not Dad's thing, though. Melting glaciers, you know, greenhouse gases causing global warming and all that? That's what Dad's into."

Paris sits up with his head and paws on the bench between Tyler and me. "You sure are a friendly guy. Been around people too much for sure." Tyler gives me a look, icy and somehow riveting at the same time. "Bet the surveyors fed him."

"What? They fed a puppy and just left him?"

"Well, what exactly can you do with a wolf? Are you staying up here forever?" Tyler asks.

"Oh gosh, no. I'm joining my mother in Paris in September."

"Well, see. You'll leave him behind too. And this guy's already had too much human contact. He probably can't go back in the wild. But he belongs in a reserve at least."

"*You* belong in a reserve." I glare at him. "You're not a wolf, are you, boy?" I scratch roughly behind Paris's ears and under his chin, and he lets out this yowl that makes me pause.

"Did you check out our 'Animals in Their Natural Habitat' display? There's a wolf in there that could be your dog's twin."

I look down at Paris and he looks back at me with his sharp yellow eyes. 'Course, the eyes in the display wolf were glassy, beady eyes.

"Why don't you check on the Internet? There'll be plenty more facts on wolves there."

I look back into glacier eyes. "Maybe you forgot. You banned us from all contact with the outside world."

The skin around Tyler's mouth buckles as he smiles. It doesn't look like he takes me seriously. "Your important e-mail—by any chance, was it from a boyfriend? Let me guess, from the city?" The way he says "city" implies some kind of fault, as though it's the city that makes a person not return e-mail.

"Why, does Parks Canada need to know this for some reason?" This Tyler guy is annoying. I can't stare him down. His eyes are that same blue I'll have to try to mix with my paints if I'm ever going to paint the lake. The color unnerves me and I have to look away.

"It just gives you an excuse to be snotty. I mean, if your boyfriend's just dumped you."

"Zane hasn't dumped me!" I see Dad and Martin coming toward us.

"So you don't have an excuse," Tyler says.

"Zanna, Zanna! Guess what?" Martin calls. "The guy at the hardware store says we can volunteer with Parks Canada this summer. We just have to talk to —"

"Me or my dad," Tyler interrupts, grinning the way Paris did after scoffing the stew.

CHAPTER 4

"JUST THINK ABOUT IT, ZANNA. YOU CAN'T SIT IN THE CABIN all day by yourself," Dad says as Martin heads into the Park Information Office with Tyler. Paris tugs at the rope, wanting to follow them. "I have to collect my ice samples. Do my research."

I yank the rope, roll my eyes, and fold my arms across my chest, the rope still tucked tightly in my fist. Paris yips his disappointment. I say nothing.

"Listen, your mother told me you need forty hours of volunteer work if you want to graduate back in the city. This is something you can do right here, right now, in Last Chance."

The Park Office door squeaks as Martin pushes it open, waving some forms. "We're all set. We just have to fill these out and Dad has to sign them."

"Or if you really don't want to volunteer, you could come up the mountain with me. Help me drill through ice, check the temperatures, and take measurements. We could have some quality bonding time." Dad winks.

I scrunch up my mouth. They're ganging up on

me, pressuring me. Will I never be able to do what I want again? "Do you expect us to hike to the office? It's miles away."

"Tyler drives a truck and says he can pick us up," Martin pipes in. "Just think, you can use the Park Office computers every day."

My eyes open wide. A lift from Tyler. I can't help smiling: at least he'll be inconvenienced too. And Martin's right: I can picture myself in a forest ranger's outfit sitting at a desk, downloading e-mail, and messaging all day long. What ever happens in a small outpost anyway? Maybe I can even make a few long-distance calls when no one's looking. "Fine, Martin. Give me that form. And take the dog." I pass him the rope. "Dad and I are spending some serious together-time grocery shopping."

Paris strains at his makeshift leash again, hacking as he chokes himself. He just wants to go far and fast, a good match for Martin, who runs everywhere just for the fun of it. They both start loping down the cracked sidewalk. A boy and his...wolf? I shake my head: nah, can't be.

Dad and I head next door to Food Village. I pick a cart from the front and push it directly to the back, past the toys, books, toothpaste, medicine, shampoo, and detergent, scouting for the deli section or maybe the international counter. Can't find either.

I double back to the front, through the clothing aisle. Dad's in there looking at a Last Chance moose hat, opening and closing the snout that forms the front of the cap. In front of him is a display of kids' pajamas, ladies' sweat suits, and unisex rubber rain boots: Last Chance fashion. No art supplies anywhere, and certainly no canvases.

"Excuse me, Miss?" I ask the only cashier standing at a register. A tall, earthy type covered in splotchy freckles, she looks up from a *Country Life* magazine. It looks like she belongs in the magazine.

"Where do you keep the pesto and the fresh pasta?"

The cashier smiles and swings her thick, orange braid back. "Gord at the back there, he's the only pesto we keep hanging around. Spaghetti's in aisle four."

I smile at her little joke because, well, I need her on my side right now if I want anything civilized to eat. "Do you stock any tofu, or soy products?"

She smiles bigger and shakes her head.

"Hummus?"

"Canned chickpeas in aisle four, right across from the spaghetti. You can mash 'em with garlic and a little Skippy peanut butter, and away you go."

"Dog food?" I wince, wondering what kind of raw state that might come in.

"Aisle four."

"Thank you! What do vegetarians do around here?"

"Pine needles are great right now. Taste like oranges." She chuckles, but this time I can't even force a smile. She shrugs her shoulders. "Fresh vegetables are in that last aisle. We're kind of low. The truck will come in tomorrow. But we have plenty of frozen corn, peas, and that fancy stir-fry stuff in the freezer section right next to them at the back."

I cruise aisle three too, just in case: pickles, vinegars, flour, cake and muffin mixes, bread, and kitchen utensils.

In aisle four, I pick up a few cans of chickpeas, and brown and black beans—only one brand to choose from. Honestly, there are more kinds of dog food. Dad joins me. "What do we get, Dad? Lamb and rice, chicken and liver, beef and kidney? Canned food, dry food, meaty round burgers?" I make a face.

"This one here." He grabs a large bag with a puppy on it. Only that puppy is a lap-size, golden brown, floppy spaniel.

I wonder if it will be enough for a dog like Paris. It's not like he's going to enjoy my table scraps.

"What do wolves eat?" I ask Dad, remembering the stuffed one in the display, teeth bared in an ugly snarl. He looked like he enjoyed rabbit sushi.

"Wolves are carnivorous pack animals that can often gang up on quite large prey."

"Humans?"

"No, never. Red Riding Hood is just a fairy tale, believe me. Mostly wolves eat field mice or beavers. Occasionally they may try their luck at a moose. "Why do you ask?"

"Oh, no particular reason." Can a wolf survive on puppy chow? I shake my head. Honestly, who cares? Someone will claim him any day now.

I make a U-turn back to the veggie aisle for that fancy stir-fry stuff. Three bags ought to do it. I meet Dad at the cash. "You bought some pasta and milk last trip in, right?"

Dad nods. He pays for the stuff and the cashier introduces herself, guessing that we are the people who moved into one of the Skylon cabins. Does everyone know what everyone else does in Last Chance?

It's a very tiny world. Turns out the cashier is Joyce Benson, somehow related to Tyler, I'm guessing. No wonder she laughs at my groceries. Making fun of city tastes runs in the family.

Back at the car, Dad tells me to fill out the form before we head back home. "I can sign it right away. No need to make another trip if you've decided." Dad sticks the box of groceries in the back, and I use the hood to write on.

Last name first, first name last, easy enough. Address and phone number, harder. References—I don't know anyone in this town. Skills—I mark down "computer."

Dad scrawls his signature at the bottom. I head back into the office.

Tyler smirks as I hand him the volunteer sheet.

"Okay, okay, I don't know my address. I don't have a telephone..."

"Don't worry about it." He writes in "Skylon cabin." Beside "References" he writes down his own name. "You're in. Do you want to start right away?"

"Oh, I would, really I would, but remember I brought my wolf?"

"Right. Pick you up at eight tomorrow?" Tyler points his pen at me.

"Eleven or twelve would work better for me."

He wags the pen. "Way too late. Have to be at the office by the afternoon. Eight or nothing."

I'm confused. It's not that far to our cabin by car. Why does he need to start off so early? Then I wonder about time in general. Is Toronto ahead of Alberta or behind? Maybe that's why there's no e-mail from Zane. Early tomorrow morning would be almost afternoon back in the city. I would be sure to hear something from him by then. "Eight o'clock it is."

Tyler's cool blue eyes hold mine for a moment, laughing at me. Lucky I have a boyfriend or that look would rattle me. I turn around and bump into Martin coming back to hand in his volunteer form too.

We say our good-byes and make our way back to the truck, where Paris is riding shotgun. "Move it," I tell him, and find I have to use all my strength to push the puppy toward the back with Martin.

I'm in a way better mood than when we first arrived here, and I switch on the radio and push the scan button. It picks up static, more static, the forest-fire-danger update for the park, some more static, and country music. I sing along. Hey, we live in the country now. When in Last Chance, you do as the desperate people do. I'll show that Tyler guy that I'm not a city snot. Martin sings along too. *My baby left me for a bodybuilder. She didn't want to live with a pipe welder.* We sound pretty awful, just like when we were kids and sang "Old Macdonald" together. Paris's head pokes forward between the front seats and his paws push up on the console. He sneaks forward.

Suddenly Dad brakes, and Paris stumbles and scrambles back onto my lap, ears pointing up like antennae, eyes sharp and trained. Ahead of us an elk strolls across the road, but it's the creature at the side of the road that gets my attention.

It looks like a large dog that's been through hard times. He's a dark-gray color with some black and brown. His long, thick tail curls unhappily between his hind legs. His eyes focus on the elk with the intensity of two yellow lasers.

"Look over there!" Martin nudges me and points. In the bushes, there are a couple more mangy-looking dogs.

"Wolves," Dad calls, "out hunting."

Paris's body feels hard and stiff as he stares at the elk. A growl rattles through his body. Is that your mom and dad? I want to ask. But he's not looking at the wolves, just at the meal on hooves.

Some noise or smell alerts the elk, and he lifts his legs and lopes off. The wolves scramble after. Paris yips and yaps; his body trembles. Now he sees the wolves, but he doesn't react any differently than one dog would acknowledging another.

Dad certainly doesn't notice any resemblance or for sure he would have mentioned it.

Once the animals leave, he starts the truck moving forward again. Does the elk make it away, do the wolves go hungry? It's another story without an ending.

When we arrive back at the cabin, the sunlight is failing. The mountains and lake turn an inky purple in the distance, but the water close to the shore is still that same Mediterranean blue. I decide there's something I have to try right away before all the light disappears. I look around for paper and finally, in desperation, I rip off May and June from the girlie calendar in the kitchen—it's July already—and stick the pages on my easel. Then I bring the whole thing closer to the lake.

First I paint over the girl in the bathing suit, Miss May. The page is glossy and the paint slides across; at least it doesn't soak right through as it might with plain paper. Then I squeeze out some blue on a palette, add a bit of white, and stir it up with my brush. I dab my brush across the paper and frown. I fill the paper with different blues. The color's not quite right. I flick some white on to get the effect of the sunlight speckled over the lake. I shake my head. I add yellow flecks. Better, but the color's not quite there yet. I whip off that page, toss it to the side, and paint over Miss June. This time I paint yellow eyes, and surround them with white hearts and black and brown markings.

Paris, clearly. I step away and the yellow eyes stare back at me, powerful and intense as lasers. He's just a big puppy dog, really, but that stare is as fierce as a wolf's.

CHAPTER 5

THAT NIGHT, I TRY TO FALL ASLEEP IN THE BLACKEST DARKNESS I've ever seen. Over my brother's breathing, I hear Paris pacing at the foot of our stairs, toenails *click-clicking* against the wooden floor, back and forth. He whimpers and I can't believe he doesn't wake my brother. Or is Martin just pretending to sleep? With our new curtain wall and in the velvety blackness of the night, I can't see Martin's face. I miss that suddenly. Maybe I should just wake him. Keeping the dog was his idea after all; why should I get up to look after Paris? When I finally have to go to the bathroom anyway, I head down the stairs.

Paris leaps to the door, howling, and I follow and slide the glass door open. No need: there is no door there anymore, only swirling masses of mist. Paris continues to cry, yet walks into it. His howl draws out longer now. First it starts off low, and then it reaches for the moon and then it drifts down again.

"Mom," he seems to cry. "Come back for me."

"It's okay, Paris. I'm here for you," I tell him but he makes me feel sad and lonely too, and he's way too far ahead to hear me anyway. I swim through the mist to join him, my arms waving it away, pushing it back. "Paris, Paris!"

"Zanna, Zanna? Is that you?" Someone calls back in a voice that caresses me with its soothing tones. It's her. My mom is somewhere out there. Suddenly I know I have to part all of the mist to find not just the dog, but Mom as well. Where is she? How far away? I walk and walk, feeling cold and confused. "Mom, Mom. I need you!"

The mist spins away and suddenly the sunlight blinds. When my eyes adjust, I see Mom sitting at a round table with Zane, beneath a patio umbrella. Both of them have their backs to me. What are they doing, talking together? They seem to be in their own world, happy without me, conspiring even. I'm so mad. I run to them and grab Mom by the shoulder, spinning her around. She has no face. "What's happening?" I scream, but no sound comes from my mouth. I grab Zane. "Help me!" I have to force him to turn too, and when he does, he's the same. His face is blank.

I gasp and sit up in bed. Just a nightmare. I can't catch my breath.

"Breathe, Zanna, breathe!" Martin has drawn back the curtain and talks to me. But I still hear snoring—Paris, slumped beside him on the bed. "Was it a bad one?"

"It was awful. Mom had no face. How did you know I was dreaming? Did I wake you?"

"Yeah. I mean no—the dog needed to go out. He's also pretty lonely. I think he misses somebody. Do you want to switch beds?"

"That's ridiculous. I'm too old to believe your bed has special immunity from nightmares."

"Too bad, because it does." Martin grins at me. "But also it contains one really large teddy bear who needs company. And he'll keep your nightmares away for sure."

The thing is, when I have a nightmare, it circles in my head the whole night. If I don't try something, I know I'll be visiting the zombies, Mom and Zane, again and again and again. I sigh. "Yeah, let's switch." We stand up and shuffle around each other.

"Skootch over, Paris." I nudge the furry, dozing animal, and he gives me a sleepy lick. "Yuck. Don't get too used to this. You should be sleeping outside," I warn him. But as I lie back down, he curls himself close to me, his head a heavy lump across my chest. Eyes closed and breathing peacefully, he makes me feel safe and warm. After a minute, I fall asleep too.

Way too early next morning, sunlight brightens the room, so it's impossible to sleep in, even if I didn't have to worry about Tyler coming. Paris licks my face as though it's a dog lollipop. "Stop that, Paris. Go visit

Martin." But of course, Martin's up already. I smell
the most tantalizing aroma and hear sizzling that
makes my mouth water, despite the fact that I'm a
vegetarian. Is there anything that smells or sounds
better than bacon cooking?

Since today is the first day I'm volunteering, I
go through my suitcase looking for my most sophisti-
cated casuals. Yesterday Tyler saw me after seven days
of living in a truck. Today he'll see me refreshed and
dressed in big, city fashion. He'll be sorry he ever gave
me a hard time. I rub at my gritty eyes. On second
thought, maybe I won't be that refreshed. I stuff my
underwear and other clothes into drawers. Aw, and
here it is, city-slick chick gear: short-short black den-
ims with large pockets and a vest to match, also with
a lot of pockets, plus an apple-red T-shirt. I pull out
a floppy black Australian bush hat and carry my entire
outfit downstairs to the bathroom to put myself together
in some kind of appealing way.

"Hurry up, eggs are ready!" Dad pounds on the
bathroom door almost the moment I step into the tub.
I shower enough to feel soggy, towel off quickly, and
throw on my clothes. With a little gel in my palms, I
scrunch up my hair into casual curls. This time
Martin pounds on the door. "Hurry up. Toast just
popped."

No time for big eye makeup. I leave the mirror for

the kitchen, climb up on a stool, and eat. The eggs
taste great. Dad's a way better cook than Mom. One
perfectly crisp bacon strip curls temptingly on a
plate in the center of the counter. I want it so badly.
But it used to be part of some cute little pig, I remind
myself. Dad ladles some brown beans next to my
eggs and passes me a slab of toasted French bread.

"Mmm." Dad snags the bacon. "Have to hand it to
you, Zanna. So much willpower. I think I could give
up any other kind of meat except bacon."

My lip twitches as I watch him chew. He's done
me a favor, really he has. Pigs deserve to live too.
The beans taste sweet and sour at the same time,
the bread thick and crunchy with a liquid layer of
warm butter. Mom and I usually have a bowl of
muesli with yogurt in the morning. I love these eggs
but have to wonder what Mom's having in Paris.
Croissants and café au lait?

"Well, I'm off. Zanna, pick up your pajamas from
the bathroom floor. Martin, clear the plates and put
them into the dishwasher. I want to get to the top
of the mountain today. Scout around before my
students get here."

"Hey, I'd like to come too," Martin says. "You
always say it's not safe to travel alone in the wilderness."

"I won't be." Dad's mouth does a quick scrunch but

he continues. "You promised you'd volunteer. You need those hours for school too. Besides, you said you missed your sister, so enjoy her while she's here.

Zanna, help your brother with the dishes."

Missed me? So it wasn't only me. We've seen each other twice in the past four years, once last September. When I got chicken pox at twelve in Toronto—the only kid in the class and right before grad—Martin got chicken pox in Yellowknife, the only kid in his class. Mom told me about it after. Might have been nice to have chicken pox together, or to celebrate our birthday in the same place at least.

"You can do the frying pan," Martin calls, "since I put all the plates in the dishwasher."

"Dishwasher," I repeat to myself, happy at this hitherto-undiscovered bit of civilization in the cabin. I scoop my sleep duds from the bathroom and fling them up to my room. It takes a few tries and, just as my pajama bottoms land, I hear honking. From the bathroom window, I can see the green Park truck on the dirt road out back. So much for cleaning that pan.

"Time to go, Martin." I rush to put my sneakers on fast and that's when I realize what Paris ate for breakfast.

"Oh my gawd! My Paluzzis!" I pick up my drooly, wet, open-faced sneakers. "What am I going to wear now?"

"Don't you have any other shoes?" Martin asks.

I sniff, thinking sad thoughts about my New York footwear. Why didn't the stupid animal find Dad's work boots flavorful? "I'll go upstairs and get my flip-flops." When I get back down, Martin and Paris are standing there waiting.

"What are we going to do about the dog?" Martin asks.

"First thing we're going to do is post a notice on the bulletin board at Food Village. Somebody must be missing this animal!" I flip-flop to the door in disgust.

"No, Zanna. I mean now. He's not allowed in the Park Office."

"He can stay outside. I'll put his dishes out there." I double back to the kitchen and carry the bowls from there to the balcony. If he's a wolf, that's where he'd normally spend all his time—outside, I mean, not on the balcony.

Tyler honks his horn again.

"So you stay around the cabin and behave your-self," I tell Paris, who, head tilted, watches my lips move. "Don't look at me like that. In the city we'd have to tie you up."

Martin runs for the truck, and Paris makes a break down the stairs after him.

"Paris! Paris, come back here!"

"Leave the dog," Tyler calls. "Once we drive off, he'll get the picture."

Martin climbs in and sits next to Tyler. I pull on the Australian bush hat and head for the truck too.

"What are you wearing?" Tyler asks me, with less admiration than I'd hoped. "What does it look like? Honestly." I glance down at myself, wondering what could be wrong. "Shorts, nothing too fancy. All right, the vest is just an accessory, but I can take it off if it gets too hot. Besides, don't we have to change into a Park uniform?"

"We don't give out uniforms to volunteers."

"Fine. You don't like shorts in the office. What do you want me to wear? I don't think I even brought a dress."

"Long pants and sleeves would be better, but I'm talking shoes here. You can't wear those!" He points to my bare feet. "Look! Your ankle is already bleeding."

"That's a strawberry and you know it," I tell him.

"What?" He squints and then breaks into a grin. "So it is. Still, you can't hike in beachwear."

"Who said anything about hiking?"

"My volunteers are doing trail work today."

"Volunteers? Are there more of us?" I ask. Maybe there's someone else our age in this burg.

"No. *You* are my volunteers."

I squint unbelievingly at him. "Whatever! The dog ate my sneakers. It's either these or my platforms."

"Never mind. I've got steel-toed boots in the back. You'll have to wear those." He leans back and throws me some dusty, yellow, mid-calf work shoes. "Now where are you going?"

I take the ugly footgear. "Back to change into jeans: long pants and long sleeves, like you said." Boots with shorts look ridiculous, after all. I walk back toward the cabin, Paris at my heels. Besides changing, I slip on two pairs of socks to make the boots fit. I take some extra time to put on mascara and eyeliner. It makes me feel better about my lumber jack feet. Fifteen minutes later, I climb up next to Martin in the truck, pushing Paris down and out. "Go home!" I slam the door quickly.

"About time." Tyler's blue eyes lock on to mine for a second. His lips tuck into a smile. He's going to say something about the eye makeup, I know he is. I dare him to, inside my head. "That's much better," he finally says and faces the road. The truck pulls away, spraying dirt over Paris. I check the side mirror.

"Paris is following."

"He'll give that up in a minute," Tyler says.

After five minutes, he's still loping near the back of the car, tongue lolling from his goofy grin.

"Wow, that dog sure can run," Martin says.

I groan. Paris will never give up. I watch him in the side mirror. This dog ate my Paluzzis. I hate him. Who cares if he kills himself on the road? But in my head I hear him howling in my dreams again and can't stand it. I lean over and punch Mountain Boy's arm. "Pull over and let the dog in."

The truck stops dead in the center of the dirt road. Tyler rubs his arm as he turns to eyeball me again. He sighs. "All right, I guess if we're working on the trails, it's okay if the wolf tags along."

"Thank you." I fling open the door and Paris jumps in happily.

"Wolf?" Martin repeats, smiling and wide-eyed. Paris leaps into my lap now, claws digging at the tops of my jeans, head up, eyes keen and trained on Tyler.

"Oh, come on. You didn't notice that your dog looks a bit...let's say, scruffy?" Tyler asks Martin.

"No. Cool, wow. My own wolf."

"But that's the problem. You're not supposed to own a wolf. He belongs out in the wild."

I make a face and look around. "What? Does it get any wilder?"

Tyler shrugs his eyebrows, and there's that smirk again. Mr. Good Looks knows it all.

I pull my hat down so he can't see my eyes. "Don't worry. We're going to find his owner somehow. Just as soon as we get into town."

Tyler spins up dirt again as we take off. A few minutes later he parks the truck in a small lot near a sign that reads *Grizzly Bear Trail.* Ours is the only vehicle and, like everything in Last Chance, the spot feels lonely and deserted. There are some rocks, some straggly shoots of grass, and a few scruffy pine trees. In the distance, the mountains look blue until they touch the clouds, where they are frosted with snow. Like a fairyland.

"We're here," Tyler says. There's a large map on a bulletin board right beside the trail sign, and a small box, into which he stuffs a stack of fliers.

"Oh man, there are bears here," Martin announces, like it's an exciting ride on a roller coaster.

I'm not as excited. Instead I read the notice about what to do if you encounter one. You're not supposed to look it directly in the eyes, and you're supposed to talk quietly so as not to scare it. If you're in a group, you should stay together to look more imposing.

Well, that's kind of contradictory. One moment you're not supposed to intimidate the bear, the next you're supposed to look threatening.

Back away slowly. You can't outrun a bear. Don't climb a tree unless you can get higher than thirty-three feet. Keep your dogs away from bears. Unless they're well trained, they lead the bear back to you.

"Tyler, what about Paris? He's not well trained."

I point to the sign.

He pats a can sticking out of his pocket. "We won't need it. But just in case, I brought spray."

Martin perks up. "Bear repellent? Shouldn't we put some on now?"

"No." He chuckles. "It's like mace. You spray it at the bear, not on yourself. But you better hope you can get it right in its eyes from close up."

"Gotcha. Should we find a stick so that we can scare the bear away instead?" He's looking around in the bush already, happy with that idea. "In case we meet one, I mean."

"Never mind. I have just the thing for both of you," Tyler answers and hands us each a long metal pick. "Your mission is to clean up garbage on this trail." He also hands us each a large green plastic bag.

"Yes, yes—this is exactly what I want to do with my summer," I tell the taller fir trees surrounding us.

"Well, if you don't want to pick up garbage, I'll let you have my job," Tyler says.

"Okay. Anything's better than picking up garbage."

He passes me a shovel and a zip lock bag.

"Congratulations, you now get to pick up scat samples."

"Scat samples?"

"He means you scoop poop," Martin tells me.

"Ew—why would anyone want to do that?" I hand

him back his tools and take the garbage pick again.

"We label the samples with where we found them, and the researchers use the DNA to study the wildlife. In this case, bears. We'll be able to tell how your father's ski development will affect the animals."

"Oh, please. My father's ski development."

"Dad works for the government and the university," Martin jumps in. "He's documenting the retreat of Ribbon Glacier and studying the effects of pollutants on the ice." Oh man, Tyler's got him on a roll now. "Did you know that the layers of a glacier are like the rings of a tree? Dad says they provide a history of the environment."

I cough now to let Martin know he's running on. He takes the hint.

"In any case, I don't understand why you think he's linked to a ski development."

"Because you live in one of those nice little chalets that belong to Skylon."

I take over now. "Let's get something straight. I think tourism is great. Probably pays for your job." I stab a pop can with my pick, then shake it loose into my green bag. "But my dad, as sickening as I think this trait may be, is pure. He's here for research and that's it."

"Whatever!" Tyler uses a high, girly pitch that I assume can only be meant as an imitation of me.

CHAPTER 6

GRIZZLY BEAR TRAIL IS SIX KILOMETERS LONG AND SHOULD take three hours to hike, according to the trail billboard. I make up my mind that it will be a lot faster. I'm going to fill this garbage bag to the top in record time. Then I can get to the Park Office e-mail.

We start off with Tyler in the lead, followed by me, Martin, and Paris in the rear. As the path meanders through small pine trees, I scan the ground looking for litter. Nothing, nothing, nothing. A spicy evergreen smell tingles in my nostrils, making my eyes squeeze together as I sneeze a couple of times. With the third sneeze, I slam into Tyler, who has stopped for some reason. "Excuse me."

"*Gesundheit.*" Tyler spins around with a smile on his face, catching my elbows in his hands. *City kids are allergic to fresh air*, his smirk says.

I smile back and point to a pile of dung on the ground about a centimeter away from his foot. "Don't you need that sample?"

He lets my arms drop as he steps away from it, shaking his head. "I'd say it's black Labrador or German Shepherd." Tyler doesn't scoop it and Paris

enjoys sniffing around the mound for a maddeningly
long time.

"Come on, Paris. Honestly." I rustle my garbage
bag at him, which makes his ears shoot up and his
body lunge forward. "Easy, boy!"

But it isn't my bag he's really after. Ahead of me
there's a rattling in the bush. Paris bolts past me and
Tyler, hurtling into the undergrowth.

Martin's face lights up. "Maybe it's a bear!" He
chases after the dog, waving his pick with one hand
and pushing away branches with the other.

"Don't go after him!" Tyler yells. "It's probably
nothing," he tells me as he reaches into his pocket
for his bear repellent.

A can of hair spray is what it looks like. How can
anything that small help us against anything as big
as a grizzly? "He's my brother and I have to look after
him," I say, and I dash into the bush too, the branches
scratching my arms and legs. At least I have a
weapon, not some wimpy spray. I grip my garbage
pick tightly. Listening for Paris's snarls and yips, I
break through to where my brother and Paris stand.
No bear anywhere, just a high-pitched chirping coming from the top of a tree.

"It's a squirrel. Cute, eh?" Martin asks.

I look up at the creature. Alert black eyes stare
back, ears and tail stand at attention, and the tiny
nose twitches. Smaller than our Toronto gray squir-
rels, it has reddish-brown fur that stands up like pine

needles. "C'mon guys, you're scaring the thing half to
death." I pull my brother back toward the path.
"Paris," I snap my fingers. "Come!"

Unbelievably the dog follows, for a while. Then he
takes off into the brush again.

"You're lucky that was a squirrel," Tyler lectures
as we walk. "Didn't you read the bear warnings?
You're not supposed to get close to them. They're
dangerous."

My smiley-faced brother listens to Tyler, but I
don't know if anything sinks in. He reminds me of the
dog in that way.

"Can we just go?" I ask. "It's almost 9:30 and I
only have one pop can." I march ahead to give them
the idea. My boots anchor me down, the metal toes
heavy as cement. Still, I move fast. "We have a job,
let's get on with it."

"Shouldn't we wait for Paris?" my brother asks.

"He'll find us, don't worry," Tyler answers.

He's right, we can't wait for the animal forever; the
hike is taking too long as it is. I walk on, staring at
the ground, willing my eyes to find garbage. Nothing. I
walk quicker till I'm out of breath. My toes feel like
they've been pummeled by hammers. Paris bounds
back onto the path and, after a few moments, heads
off into the trees again. We pass by four information
posts and don't see one speck of litter, but Paris leaps
onto the path at regular intervals, almost as though
he's checking on us. "Did you just make up a job to

keep us busy?" I complain as we approach post five.

"No, this is routine maintenance. And it's not some kind of race. Have a seat and rest." Tyler points out the bench and sits down himself.

"That one's mine!" I call to Martin as I stab an old, empty cigarette pack and shake it into my garbage bag.

Martin's not interested in picking up litter anyway. At every sound or twitch of a leaf, he glances around as if expecting something. Sharp, quick, ears up, almost like Paris. Frowning, he opens a Park flier. "Post five," he says. "Let's see. Plant life," he reads. Apparently the trees surrounding us are lodgepole pine and alder.

I look around: one tree's pretty much the same as the next to me. They're shaggy and green.

"Nothing about bears here." His shoulders sink.

"Doesn't matter," Tyler says. "Bears don't read. And they often come down this low to find grass shoots and horsetails."

As if to demonstrate his point, a branch snaps and the bushes suddenly shake. I gasp, then jump as the branches and leaves part.

Paris tumbles out. My brother and Tyler laugh.

I take deep breaths to slow my heartbeat back down again.

Something hangs from Paris's mouth. Yeak! It's moving—a snake, alive and wriggling. "Get it out of his mouth!" I yell at Martin.

"He's not hurting it. Come here, boy!" Martin wrestles Paris to the ground and forces his jaw open. The snake slithers a hasty getaway. Paris races back into the brush.

"Bad dog, stop!" I yell after him.

"What's your problem?" Tyler asks. "He's just obeying his natural instincts."

"Look, I never even wanted a dog. This one ate my favorite shoes for breakfast. Now he's hunting snakes for lunch. The faster we find his owner, the better."

"There's always the wolf reserve." Tyler shrugs. "Speaking of lunch, did you pack one?"

"I wasn't talking about lunch. I was talking about Paris, who's a dog, not a wolf."

"We didn't have time to make sandwiches," Martin answers for me.

"That's okay. I brought extra. We can sit up at my favorite spot by the creek and have a picnic."

"Picnic? Here? Aren't we almost done yet? Can't we have lunch in town? I've got money."

"The Charcoal Pit's closed today. The only other place serving lunch is Food Village, which is where my sandwiches came from."

"Darn. I wanted to eat out."

Tyler opens his arms to the forest around us. "You are." My brother and Tyler chuckle at each other. They're ganging up on me too, just the way Martin does with Dad.

I fold my arms across my chest.

"Don't be mad," Tyler says. "Wait till you see the view from my spot. No restaurant could match it."

I sigh, and we walk on forever. Post six mentions ferns. Post seven describes the bearberry, which is the grizzly bear's favorite fruit in the springtime. I'm so bored. In my head I hear that stupid country song again: *My baby left me for a bodybuilder. She didn't want to live with a pipe welder.* The same chorus repeats itself, making me crazy. What is the next line?

For no reason, Martin suddenly breaks into song: "I've got the tools, he hangs around pools. I need to get a six-pack if I want my baby back. Oooooh!"

A shiver runs up my spine. He knows what I'm thinking; after four years apart, Martin can still finish my thoughts...and the songs running in my head. He sings the next verse and I sing along.

Suddenly Tyler squats and pulls out a small hand shovel from his pack.

The song stops. "What is that?" Martin drops down beside him and a large mound of what looks like coal lumps. Martin's so excited I swear he wants to drop down and sniff everything, like Paris. "Is it bear scat?"

I peer over his shoulder and wrinkle my nose.

"Yup," Tyler answers, and begins scooping some into a plastic bag.

"So where is the bear? How come we never see any?" Martin looks around.

"This isn't a zoo, Martin." Tyler zips up the bag

and marks the date and place across it. "They come and go freely—the way your wolf should."

"Speak of the devil; where is the stupid dog?" It hits me like a punch that I haven't seen or heard him in a while. I remember my drooly, shredded sneakers in the next breath. "Serve him right if a bear eats him." I cup my hands around my mouth and call. "Paris!" Still no rustling in the bush to signal his return. No sound at all. That's weird. "Paris!" I didn't mean it about a bear eating him, really I didn't. Having said it, though, I start imagining it. Paris bounding up to a big grizzly bear, tail wagging, grin across his face. The bear swiping at him with a massive paw. Paris yelping. I start calling, crazy, frantic; he's just a puppy, after all. "Pa-riiiiiis!" Nothing. "Oh, where is he?"

Martin puts two fingers in his mouth and whistles, a long, high-pitched note. Still nothing, for a moment, and another and another. Then suddenly the brush rips open and Paris leaps onto the path in front of us.

I let my head slump forward on my chest and sigh as I rub my temples.

I can see Tyler's smile from the side of my eye. "Bears avoid people if at all possible. Unless you separate a mother from her cub, chances are, even if you bump into one, it will just take off."

"Yes, except we're traveling with a very annoying dog. And I read the bear rules on that one."

Tyler scratches the top of Paris's head roughly.

"You don't have to worry. No self-respecting bear would tangle with this guy. Not if she could help it."

I'm not reassured. I shake my garbage bag. "I'm never going to fill this. There's no litter anywhere."

"Good! It's early in the season. Here, give me that thing." Tyler snatches my garbage pick from me too.

"Will you do me a favor and look up? Come on, we're almost at the creek. You'll like it."

My hands feel empty, and at first I swing them as I walk. The monotony of the trees and brush is boring, but it's relaxing too. I stop swinging and breathe deeply. There aren't any insects, and it's the perfect temperature for a hike: not hot enough to feel sticky or cold enough to need a jacket. I slow down my stride. Beneath my steel toes, the earth feels spongy with brown soil and pine needles. Tall cedars form a dark cave around us: a cozy room in the wild openness of the mountains. I feel more secure. Martin must feel it too—he's not singing or reading every signpost. Doesn't look as though he's bear-hunting either.

The rhythm of my feet and the silence make me slide into a no-thought mind-melt, sort of like the yoga Mom and I used to do together in the days when we were talking. Somewhere beyond the trees, I hear the loud *shhh, shhh* of water. I hear an insistent tap-tapping in the trees above my head, and look way up to where the sound is coming from. A woodpecker.

It's large, almost crow-size, and black with a red cap on its head. I inhale deeply and glance toward Tyler.

"What kind of bird is that? It's huge," Martin asks.

Tall and self-assured, Tyler nods. "That's a pileated woodpecker. They mate for life."

Know-it-all. I feel like arguing with him. "Where's its partner then? Maybe they mate forever but can't stand to be together."

"So cynical. Even in the city, I'm sure married couples work apart," he answers.

"And just like in the country, they go their separate ways. No one stays together forever."

He shrugs. "Maybe."

Point scored, although I wanted him to argue with me some more. I want someone to tell me there are happily-ever-afters.

"Oh, c'mon, Zanna," Martin pipes up, a beat later. "Lots of people stay together. Grandma and Gramps. Some of the kids in my class lived with both their parents. It just doesn't work out for everyone."

Once again Martin answers a thought in my head; it's eerie, yet comforting. He sings again as we move on: *My baby left me for a bodybuilder. She didn't want to live with a pipe welder.*

The path turns and we're at post number ten, Grizzly Creek. Ahead is a bright splash of color, orange and white wildflowers, and around a bend I spot it, a milky-white stream frothing around the rocks. I stop and inhale deeply; more pine tingles up my nose, but I smile as I realize I'm not sneezing anymore. City girl wins over nature.

"This is it. This is the spot!" Tyler opens his arms wide.

Paris gallops to the water and then tries to approach it from different angles for a drink.

We follow Tyler out onto a large, flat, gray rock. Around us the foam bites at the rock as the water jumps over itself to get somewhere fast. The grass and trees are sparse here and scruffy, like at the beginning of the trail. The sky-scraping mountains tower white and godlike. No one says anything for a while.

Paris gives up on the water, comes up on the rock, and nuzzles my knee. I pat him begrudgingly.

"Okay, let's eat." Tyler breaks the silence as he sits down and removes an insulated bag from his backpack.

He tosses us each a granola bar, an apple, and a sandwich. Then he pours some canteen water onto the rock for Paris.

"Thanks, Tyler," Martin says.

"Do you always bring this much food just for yourself?" I ask.

Tyler blushes. "My stepmother packs it. When I'm out on the trails, she insists I take a lot of food just in case."

Stepmother. Wonder what happened to his real mother. Guess she wasn't the pileated woodpecker type. I take my sandwich out of a zip lock bag and peel it open.

"It's peanut butter and jam. Doesn't need refrigeration," Tyler offers.

"Good. I'm vegetarian."

"Yeah, Joyce told me."

"Who?"

"Joyce, the cashier." He shrugs. "My stepmother."

I want to sink my teeth into the sandwich no matter what it is; I'm starving. But something bothers me. "Just how close was this sandwich to your bag of bear poo?"

Tyler laughs, deep and rumbling again. "A whole other compartment."

"Glad you find me funny," I tell him as I take a bite.

"Only in a good way." He stares out at the mountains as he chews. He pushes the canteen toward me.

Martin and Paris dash after something brown, furry, and fast. So much for the lovely calm, Zen feeling I thought we were all sharing. I finish my sandwich. "Okay, well, I'm done eating. We should head off after them."

"Let them be. We don't have to go right away. Sit still for a minute."

"Actually I wouldn't mind getting back to the house soon," I yawn. "I could use a nap."

He holds out his backpack. "Lean back, use this as your pillow," he tells me.

I take off my boots and socks to give my toes some air, roll up my pant legs, and lean back as he suggests, the sun warm on my face.

"It's beautiful, but it is lonely. Not everyone can take living here." He sounds sad, and for once I don't feel like smacking him.

I close my eyes.

"It's nice to share this spot with someone."

Maybe if I weren't so tired I'd think about the lumps underneath my head in the backpack. Instead, I find myself drifting off. It's a delicious feeling, half in this world hearing the water shushing everyone, half somewhere else. I'm not even sure how long I've been lying there when I feel a tickle against my ankle. I brush at it, and my hand hits Tyler's.

I'm embarrassed at the touch. I mean, I was expecting to swat a bug and instead my hand hits his fingers. Something about Tyler makes me want to see Zane again so badly, to see him smile, to hear him laugh.

"Did it hurt much? I mean, the needle."

"What are you talking about? Did what hurt?"

"The tattoo."

"I didn't mind suffering for art. Don't you like strawberries?" I sit up.

"I don't know. My mom sure loved them."

He sounds wistful, as though he never sees her anymore. I don't know what to say. "My mom likes avocados. In salads and dips, there was always this green snotty stuff." I look at Tyler but he's staring at the water. "She won't travel with my dad on his research trips anymore. And he never stops traveling."

"And how about you? Can you take the traveling?" he asks. I shrug my shoulders, picturing my mother at the Eiffel Tower. She certainly enjoys some travel. I stand up and walk toward the rapids.

"What are you doing?" Tyler calls as he follows.

"I want to test the water," I say, picking my way down through the rocks.

"Are you crazy? It's freezing." He quickly pulls off his own shoes and socks, hopping from one foot to the other. Then he rolls up his jeans. "Don't you dare go in there alone. The current's dangerous."

As I step in gingerly, the rushing water feels like a powerful ice jet. I want to leap out screaming, but don't want to give Tyler the satisfaction. Needles shoot into my ankles until I can't feel my feet at all. I take another step.

Tyler picks his way in after me, and I watch his face screw up around a scream he won't let loose.

Martin steps out of the bush at that moment. "Hey, that's a great idea. Last one in is a rotten egg!" He kicks off his sneakers and plunges in too. "Ahh— you guys are nuts. This water is freezing." Martin hops back up the bank.

Tyler grabs my hand, and it's a warm shock. "Don't go in any further!"

The water sucks at me but Tyler's grip is strong

and when he squeezes my hand, I feel safe.

He tugs and turns. "Come on, let's go back. This is ridiculous."

I'd like to run back up the bank, but I can't let him boss me around so I take one more step forward instead, tugging him along. For one moment my heel connects with a stone, but the stone jostles loose and my heel glides over it. I flail, and then I fall.

Backward. The world splinters into shards of needle-sharp water. Up my nose, down my throat. I try to scream, but swallow more needles.

CHAPTER 7

I BUMP AND TUMBLE THROUGH THE WATER ALONG SHARP rocks, kicking my legs and waving my arms. I can't grab on to anything to stop myself. Out of breath, out of control. Frozen, numb, *bump, bump.* I swallow more icy water, try to sputter it out; choke, cough, *bump, bump,* float.

I can't feel anything from the neck down. *Bump, bump,* the rapids flip me around the other way. The current is in control. I don't even have enough feeling left to fight it. Am I up or down? Can't reach the surface. Is this it? *Bump, bump,* snag.

My neck snaps back. I've stopped tumbling but the water rushes over me. Something pulls my shirt away in the opposite direction. What's happening? What is that? I feel a stronger tug than the water, upward. I suck in air. A hand grabs my arm. "You're okay. Crawl back here, I've got you."

Tyler, wow, oh man. I gulp for more air. Thank you, thank you. He takes my hand and pulls me into the shallower water and onto the rocks.

My throat and chest hurt. I cough violently as I crawl onto the bank.

"Are you okay?" Martin asks.

I double over and hack out the icy water as he pats my back. When I can breathe again, I start laughing uncontrollably. I'm cold and wet. My butt and legs are sore from where I bumped along the rocks, and I still can't get enough air. I gulp as I laugh. I could have died back there. In just one instant, that bubbly white milk-water turned treacherous. I want to cry and never stop crying. But that would be embarrassing so I keep laughing instead.

Tyler stares at me, breathing hard. "Do you have any idea how stupid that stunt was?"

"Leave her alone," Martin tells him. "Do you have a sweater or jacket in your bag?"

My teeth start to clatter. Tears run down my cheeks. My wet T-shirt clings and I pull it from my body.

Tyler rummages through his backpack and pulls out an orange sweatshirt.

"Here, take this." Tyler's eyes are trained on my wet T-shirt. He coughs slightly: *ahem.*

I snap the orange top out of his hands and hiccup my words. "How am I going to change out here?" He shrugs. "Martin and I will look the other way. There's no one else for miles. Martin?" He points away, and they both turn.

They stand together near the rock, Paris by their side, heads and snout all pointed in one direction, away from me. It would make a cute postcard but instead of making me laugh, the tears run down my cheeks faster.

I peel off the clingy top and pull on the sweat-shirt Tyler tossed me. Deep breaths now. In. Out. I'm getting warmer, calmer. My jeans weigh me down, stiff and heavy, plastered against my legs. I put my socks on and that helps, along with Tyler's ugly boots.

Tyler turns and checks out my dry top, blushing when he realizes I've noticed.

I nearly killed myself in the water just horsing around, so I feel like the dumbest stump in the for-est. I'm glad he feels embarrassed about something too. His blush is great. It makes him less superior, and puts me more in control again.

"I better take you home so you can get out of all your wet things."

Home. I picture Zane's pale face back at the house that used to be my home, watching a com-puter screen, and realize he never blushes. He never loses control to me either. I mostly feel imma-ture and insignificant around him. Just as I usually do with Tyler. Is that why Tyler always reminds me of Zane? I blush now. I picture the place that is now home, a Heidi cabin with Dad and Martin. I sigh. "You know what—by the time we get back to the truck, these will be dry. Let's just go back to the office."

Tyler turns and starts walking, faster than before. "Of course, you're expecting an important message." There's that disapproving tone again.

What happened this time to set him off? "C'mon," he says. "We better get going."

I still feel pretty soggy by the time we arrive back at the Park Office, and I'm sneezing. We come up against the same problem as before: no pets or wolves allowed inside. That's okay, because Tyler assigns us feeding duties for the lizard and bass in the tanks on either side of the Internet computers. First step is catching insects outside.

"You go on ahead, bro," I tell Martin. "I'll join you as soon as I've checked my mail."

Paris happily trails after him. I head back to use the Internet. A minute later, Martin comes in again to borrow a rope because Paris is snapping up the insects before he can. He goes back outside to tie him to the bench.

Before I even sit down at the computer, Tyler's dad leaves with Quincy. Super Rescue Dog appears to have trouble walking. He can't even drag his hindquarters into position to stand up right.

"The vet's in town. Dad's taking Quincy to see him," Tyler explains after the Park truck leaves. Then he steps outside and hollers that Martin and Paris can come inside any time, at least until his father returns. "See, a while back, Dad got in trouble over Quincy," he says to me. "Only service dogs are allowed in the office. He argued that rescuing was a service, but since the dog's retired, they still made an issue of it. Dad feels he has to be extra strict about other animals to make up for Quincy's exemption."

"Don't worry about it. I'm going to find Paris's real owner and it won't be a problem anymore." I sit down at the computer, dial up, and go to the mailer site. Martin steps around me to throw a grasshopper in to the lizard. Paris watches the aquarium intently, ears and tail up. I look over but turn away when I notice the grasshopper frantically leaping at the glass.

"It's the food chain, Zanna. It's not like the lizard can order tofu," Martin tells me.

"Yeah, well, careful. Paris might decide lizard's on the bottom of his food chain in a second." Tyler raises an eyebrow arrow aimed in the dog's direction but I ignore them all and focus on the screen in front of me. Contact with the outside world: my body itches with anticipation, I need it so desperately.

Mail, mail, nothing. Nothing from Zane, that is. There's a couple more from Mom: *More Exciting News,* and *Call Me.* I move the cursor down to one of her messages and my finger hovers over the Enter button. I frown. I can see her and Zane so clearly sitting at the round table in my dream. They're both in civilization, where there's tofu and takeout, art canvases and unchewed designer footwear. I'm here with garbage picks and bear poop, a destructive dog, and killer white water.

I open a new e-mail message to Zane instead. It's
not his fault if the Internet provider he uses can't
connect. It's far too early to expect snail mail from
him yet.

*Hi Zane. Weather's been great here and I just
finished a six-kilometer hike with Tyler, the
park ranger.*

I write that in, thinking that maybe making Zane
a little jealous will give me some control again.

*No stores at all, but not as boring as you might
think. We saw a snake and some bear dung.
Also, I fell in the white water and nearly
drowned.*

I remember the stinging needles in my mouth and
all over my body, and the way Tyler pulled me out.
The way it was hard to catch my breath. The way
Tyler looked at my wet T-shirt.

*I'm okay though, as you may have guessed by
the fact that I am e-mailing you. And I am still
very bored. Believe it or not, there's only one
restaurant in town: the Charcoal Pit, which I'm
guessing barbecues hunks of animal flesh,
since the only vegetarian food available is
peanut butter and artificial peanut butter. Do*

*you have any idea how much I miss you? I love
you Zane XXXOOOO P.S. Please write soon as I
am dying to hear from you. Mom bet me that
we would never last and we can't let her win!!!*

I press *Send* and once again double-check for
more e-mail. Another note drops down from Mom:
Last Chance. I hesitate. No, no, I must be strong.
I will not communicate with that woman; she has to
pay for banishing me to Last Chance.

Still, how does she like Paris? Is it everything we
ever dreamed about? Is she painting tons? Do they
like her art over there? Does she want to send for
me? Would she want to send for me if she knew I had
just nearly drowned?

I quickly exit from the Internet before I give in to
curiosity. Martin feeds the large bass on the other
side of me now, and Paris, well, he's gnawing at one
of my feet again, enjoying the flavor of Tyler's work
boots. "Stop that! Tyler, can I use this computer to
make my "Found" poster for the dog?"

"No, that one's not connected to the printer. Come
around here."

"You can't do that, Zanna. Paris is my dog!"
Martin complains.

"If he doesn't have another owner, you have nothing to worry about, do you?" I walk over to the office
side of the counter, "And if he does, then he was
never your dog to begin with." Tyler pulls out a chair

for me and I sit down, opening up a paint program on the computer. I think for a moment.

"You wouldn't have a digital camera to take a picture of him, would you? I could use it in the poster."

"Nope. Just download a picture of a wolf for the description," Tyler suggests.

"C'mon, stop, Zanna. I won't let Paris eat any of your clothes anymore," Martin begs.

"Don't worry, Martin. No one will claim him," Tyler says.

I roll my eyes and type: "Found near Skylon property." The moment I see the word Skylon, I feel disloyal. Dad would never work for developers. He's always being called away to speak about fossil-fuel emissions, and their effects on the ice caps. Building condos might not directly contribute to melting glaciers, but cutting down the trees or using up tons of hydro or water for the development would. How could Dad possibly work for Skylon? And why? But that's what the people around here call the cabins where we live. What can I do? Dad probably has no choice but to rent from them.

I continue typing. "Large puppy, gray, brown, and black, with white markings around the face and distinctive yellow eyes."

I hit another snag. We don't have a phone. How will the owner ever get in touch with us?

"Problem printing?" Tyler says when he sees me frowning, and comes over.

"We're so out of touch with the world. We don't even have a telephone in the cabin," I tell him.

"Just use the Park's. Trust me, it won't be an issue."

"And why not? You think you know everyone and everything?"

"Joyce told me the surveyors bought dog food but they never left with a dog. They can't take a wolf back to the city. I also know your dad met with one of the guys yesterday at the store."

"So?"

"Bet a Skylon surveyor went up to the glacier with your father today. They're both measuring out a nice spot for the ski resort parking lot."

"Dad goes up there to measure ice density, not spaces for parking lots," Martin tells him. "His regular crew hasn't arrived yet, that's all."

"Yes, and Dad shouldn't go up there alone. It's like swimming. You never go up a mountain without a buddy. Anyway, I'm typing *Call the Park Office If This Is Your Dog.* Can you just print it for me?"

"Sure thing. But if your dad gets use of the Skylon helicopter, we'll all know for sure."

The printer takes a minute, during which my arms are folded across my chest and no one's saying anything. When the poster rolls out, I snatch it up.

"Did you want a few more to post all around the town, or do you just want to put it up at Food Village?"

"All around the town. Wait, let me just think

about that. I think Food Village is enough. Your step-mother will spread the word." I rustle the paper. "Be back in ten."

Martin chases after me. "Do you think it's true? Is Dad really working for the bad guys?"

"Absolutely not. And nothing Ranger Boy says will ever convince me." At that moment, I spot something hovering in the air near the mountains. I squint and make out a helicopter with a machine hanging from a rope attached to it. It looks like the drill Dad uses to bore through the ice. I squint harder and read the letters on the side of the helicopter: SKYLON.

CHAPTER 8

IN THE EVENING, THE REST OF DAD'S CREW ARRIVES IN TWO trucks packed with equipment and a couple of quad-type ATVs: Drew, Jason, and Cassandra, all three his graduate students. I remember Drew and Jason from last September's visit with Dad while he was doing his teaching thing in Waterloo, and they still look the same. Drew is tall, thin, bald, and slightly geeky-looking with black-rimmed glasses. Jason's shorter and broader with curly black hair and a mustache. They both wear the standard student jeans and T-shirt. Drew accentuates his look with a vest that has a million pockets. Cassandra I don't remember meeting, and I would remember her. Girl students worship Dad more obviously than guys, so they stick out in my memory. Quiet as a snake, Cassandra's the tallest of the crew, with giraffe-long legs and tiny khaki shorts, and firm brown arms poking out of a camouflage-splotched tank top. She doesn't wear mascara, so her long eyelashes look like albino spiders. Her hair's fine and almost white too.

Paris goes crazy over her. Cassandra pitches a stick for him along the shore and he brings it back to her over and over, like a devoted servant, till she goes into the other cabin to unpack. Then Paris finally returns to us, skulking and disappointed-looking.

That's when Dad heads over to the other cabin to talk to his crew, Cassandra included. She's younger and prettier than Mom, taller and probably smarter about the stuff that's important to Dad. Here's someone who likes to live and work with ice, for sure; someone he spends more time with than Mom or me. Cassandra really annoys me.

I bang the dishes around as I clean up after supper. Paris watches. There's bean salad leftovers— Martin and Dad didn't like it much—and a few pork chops, the ones Dad made for me because he forgot I was vegetarian. And apple crisp that Martin made. He promised to show me how next time. Mom and I never cook together.

"Tell you what, dog, I'll give you all this meat on the condition that you leave the shoes alone."

Paris perks up his ears and watches my lips, or rather the frying pan in my hands. I wince as I cut up the chops. Touching dead flesh is becoming a habit for me. Quickly, I mix the pieces in with the dry dog food. Paris wolfs it down in about five seconds. Did I say *wolf*? He *dogs* it all down. He's just a normal canine enjoying some tasty table scraps. "Don't worry, your real owner will claim you."

Paris doesn't look worried, just hungry.

That night I sleep well: I hear Martin and Paris snoring in stereo, and find that comforting. No bad dreams: it's like I have a double charm to ward them off. And next morning, all our footwear looks intact. "Paris, Paris?"

I head down the stairs and find some cereal. With my bowl and a glass of milk, I head to the deck in the front. The door is already open, and by the lake Martin throws a stick for Paris.

Paris bounds after it, the only movement in view. It's so peaceful. No moose in the lake, just ghostly wisps of mist drifting up from it.

Paris snaps up the stick, but instead of returning it to my brother, runs from rock to rock, wagging his tail, bowing, inviting Martin to chase him. And Martin does, laughing. I want to run with them too, but somebody honks in the back. I turn. It's the Park truck. Tyler gets out and Paris runs toward him. I dash back in the house to chuck my bowl in the dishwasher.

Martin drifts in more slowly.

"Get a move on, Martin. We're keeping Ranger Boy waiting."

He holds a finger to his mouth. "Shhh! I'm not volunteering today. I'm going out with Dad," he whispers.

"Whatever." I dig my fists into my hips, annoyed. I hate being shushed. As I head for the truck, another feeling tingles just below my skin. Something's up. I should stay with my brother today. Go with him. "Martin!" I call back.

He ignores me. Not like him at all. I should tell Tyler to go on ahead without me. I should hang back with Martin and see what's up. Instead I head out to the truck where Tyler stands rubbing Paris's ears.

"Hey Zanna. How'd you like to take a little detour before we do our trail today? Where's Martin anyway?" Tyler looks around and over my shoulder, as if I could hide my giant, lanky brother.

"He's going out with my dad."

Tyler suddenly straightens. "Who is that?" Pure admiration shines in his voice. He waves at someone. I turn and sigh. "Cassandra, one of my father's assistants."

Cassandra grins, a big white-toothed smile, and waves back at Tyler.

I turn back. "She's got to be at least ten years older than you. Stop drooling."

"I was just being friendly."

"C'mon, you were saying something before, Tyler. Where did you want to go?"

"The wolf center; we can bring Paris along. You can see how they operate. If you like it, we can leave him there."

I hesitate. Paris hasn't destroyed anything in almost twenty-four hours, and it seems unfair to brand him a wolf again.

"Nobody's going to force you. It's just an option. I don't think your brother wants to part with Paris at all, so you'll have to be the mature one about it."

I picture Martin crashing into the bush after Paris to look for bears. Martin and that animal have a tight connection; he'd never agree to a separation. "You're right. Better to go today when he's busy." I whistle a creaky note at Paris to get his attention, and he jumps into the truck.

He sits between Tyler and me. He's big and sloppy, with his mouth hanging open in a happy pant. I scratch between his ears guiltily. We don't have to give him to anyone. Am I going soft? Paris licks at my fingers.

"The reserve is about a half an hour away. It's about fifteen acres. But the area is fenced off, so Paris wouldn't be able to run back home."

In two days, would Paris already consider the cabin his home? I try to picture the apartment building we lived in back in Toronto and have a hard time. All I can see in my mind is our Heidi cabin here in Last Chance, and it's only been two days for me too. I fold my arms across my chest and stare out at the scenery ahead of us.

It always looks rough, like the trees need a good trim or brush; maybe the mountains need straightening, polishing, or sanding, or the fields a good sweep. Green, gray, brown, scraggly, not like the clean, straight, polished angles of the skyscrapers in the city. Still, the sun is a burst of yellow light in a sky wide and blue, like some great big unblinking eye. Toronto would be hazy with smog. In the passage-

ways between them, the buildings block out the sunlight and sometimes the wind kicks up in gusts, and
mini tornados, trapped between the cement towers.

"By the way, Joyce told me she ordered some tofu
for you. Should be in next time you go for groceries,"
Tyler tells me.

"Wow, that's nice of her. Do you think I could ask
her to get some avocados for me too?"

"I don't know. They may be a little harder to
transport. You miss your mother, do you?"

He remembered what I'd said about her the other
day. "No, I don't miss her. She just turned me into
an addict. Green snot in everything, or else I feel
incomplete."

Tyler chuckles. "You'll be dipping your corn chips
in guacamole again in September. While you're in Last
Chance, you're just going to have to tough it out."

"What about you, Tyler?" I ask gently.

"I don't like avocados."

"Strawberries, I mean. When do you get to see
your mom?" I toss it off like it's no big deal.

He grips the steering wheel a little tighter. "Never.
She's dead."

I stare at his profile for a minute, debating whether
I should ask him how it happened and when, but it's
not an easy, breezy conversation. My mother sent me
away, which means she's never around for me. I make
her dead in my mind and try on how that feels, but I
can't imagine it. So we drive in silence.

After a while, Paris slumps down and puts his head on my lap to sleep, like a baby. A hairy one with yellow eyes.

The trees flash by. We turn off at a log sign that reads *Rocky Mountain Wolf Haven*. Bump, bump, over a dirt road. Paris sits up.

"The retreat usually keeps about ten wolves at a time." Tyler starts talking again. "We may not even see any unless it's feeding day."

"What do you mean, feeding day? How often do they get fed?"

"Once a week—Friday, I think—so we should be okay, 'cause they'll come right to the window then."

I put my arm around Paris and rub his head. Food once a week—Paris would starve. "Doesn't it bother them to be watched like that?"

"It's one-way glass and there's a microphone so we can hear them. They don't know any humans are there. Hey, don't look like that. They have fun. Not like real wolves who have to hunt. They eat and play and sun themselves."

"Paris loves to run."

"Fifteen acres, he'd have plenty of space and play-mates too."

I squint at Tyler. He's sure trying to sell me on this place.

When we roll into the parking lot, it sounds like a dogfight is going on. Yips, yaps, and yelps. The hairy baby jumps up, ears at attention.

"We can take him for a walk first, if you like, but we better leave him outside the observation building."

"That yapping, is that the wolves?" I ask. Tyler nods.

"I really want to see them. Let's leave Paris in the truck for now." We both roll our windows down a few inches and get out, me pushing Paris back to slam the door in his face. Paris squeezes his muzzle through the window opening.

"He can't force that open, can he?" I ask Tyler.

"No. Besides, this won't take all that long. If it does, we'll come back for him."

Inside the building, we walk quickly through a display area of wolf paraphernalia—skulls, pelts, jaws, books—to the large, glassed-in room: the observation area. I gasp when I see a wolf strolling right in front of us. White and big, he doesn't look happy like Paris. His tail is tucked between his back legs like he's been scolded. Sneaky, sneaky, he looks all around as he approaches some kind of bloody carcass.

Suddenly an even larger black wolf tears out after him and nips him. He stands by the gore, baring his teeth in an ugly, rumbling growl.

"That's Konan, the alpha male."

I jump, not expecting to hear anyone else besides Tyler in the room.

A man in a khaki uniform introduces himself. "I'm Peter Kerrigan, the retreat manager. That white wolf is Chinook. He's beta, so he's supposed to wait till Konan lets him eat."

"Not very good at sharing," I say.

A gray wolf, and a couple more that could be Paris's parents, huddle in the forest a few meters off. Looks like they're chomping on other parts of the dead beast. Gross.

"This is Zanna," Tyler gestures toward me. "Her family found a wolf cub under their cabin. He looks to be about five or six months old. Do you think it's too late for him to join your pack?"

"He doesn't stand a chance otherwise." Peter scratches his chin; he's one of those guys who grows black stubble seconds after he shaves. Or maybe he's a werewolf. "A wolf that hangs around people too much is a wolf the rangers will have to shoot later."

Is Paris really a wolf, I wonder? And if he is, hasn't he already hung around people too much?

The black wolf suddenly breaks into a run in front of us—long stride, legs out straight like wings, free. For a moment I can see how this might be perfect for Paris. Then I look down at the bloodied carcass.

"That's a deer. They quite enjoyed it," Peter tells us. Chinook approaches it again and quickly carries a leg back into the forest.

I shake my head and sit on the bench by the window, mesmerized. What is the difference between a dog and a wolf, really? I see a small gray one bend down on his front legs and wag his tail. I watch the large black one walk toward him and sniff him indulgently. The white one bends down too, and then breaks into a run.

Without reason or warning, the gray one howls, low at first, and then he raises his muzzle as the howl grows higher and louder. I can feel it in my bones.

"C'mon, Tyler, we better go check on Paris." I stand up and walk back through the skulls and pelts, forgetting to say anything to Peter.

"Call me if you have any questions," I hear him tell Tyler.

I push through the door and breathe in deep gulps of air.

"I can tell you didn't like it, but honestly, Zanna, I don't think you're thinking it through right. You can't look at things like a city person. Paris isn't some shih tzu lapdog."

"Yeah, but to have to fight for a big raw leg of a deer for his once-a-week meal? I don't know. It just seems too wild for him." At the car, I open the door and Paris hops down, rushing to the high green wooden fence separating the reserve from the rest of the parkland. Paris sniffs along it and then lifts his leg to mark his territory.

More yips and yaps make Paris lift up his ears, and there it is again, that howl—long, low, and mournful—from the other side of the fence.

My heart stops beating for a moment when Paris

lifts up his head and returns the howl, just as low, just as bone-rattling.

"C'mon, boy. Let's get our work done. You can have your walk on the Sky Mountain Trail," Tyler says and climbs back into the truck.

"Sky Mountain?" I repeat.

He nods. "Our trail maintenance for today."

I scramble out of the truck after Paris. "Hope you don't mind, I still need to borrow your boots till I can buy better shoes."

"Better order them at the hardware store if you want a particular size," Tyler suggests as he starts the drive.

Paris keeps looking back at the green fence. He jumps in the back and continues to watch the Rocky Mountain Wolf Haven disappear in the back window.

"It's like he knows someone there, eh?" Tyler suggests.

"I don't care." But I do, for some strange reason. It suddenly feels important to get Paris away from his roots. Like if I don't, he'll definitely turn into a wolf if he isn't one already. "Paris, come back here." Paris obeys and plants his long legs against the dash.

The drive to the trail only takes about fifteen minutes and I'm happy to start on another long, mindless hike, garbage pick in hand, dog scrambling ahead. The scenery feels the same as yesterday— patches of brush and wildflower a spongy pine-needle path through some taller forested area, and some gaps where sky and mountain take my breath away. The path winds higher, my breathing becomes heavier, and I wipe sweat from my brow.

Then it stops at the edge of a cliff. I inhale deeply and release my breath. Up ahead, two white mountains spike into the clouds. Down below, dizzyingly far, there's a river and more brush. My breath catches; I back away before I can be sick. Heights are not my thing.

Tyler doesn't seem to notice and continues to play tour guide. "That's Ribbon River. Leads off from the Ribbon Falls. Which come from the glacier lake."

"Ribbon Glacier?" I ask.

He grins. "None other."

"That must be where Dad and his crew are working." Paris runs into my legs hard, as if begging for a chance to see too.

"Try and keep him back," Tyler says and plucks a single blue poppy growing in a cluster a few meters away from the path. It's bright and friendly-looking, like the poppies on the divider curtain in my room. He stares straight ahead for a moment, twirling it between his fingers. His lips part and move almost as if in prayer. A feeling hangs in the air around him, a sadness, bone-aching, like the wolf howling back at the center. Otherwise I'd rib him about picking a wildflower. It's got to go against every ranger rule in the book.

I grab Paris by the scruff and hold him tight.

"Here you go, Mom," Tyler finally says, and flings the flower off the cliff.

I'm glad that for once, I kept my mouth shut.

CHAPTER 9

HAD HE REALLY SAID THAT? I RELEASE PARIS AND HE TEARS
into the trees behind us. Tyler turns and we continue
as if nothing happened. His mother is dead and he
throws flowers off the cliff for her. Does that mean she
fell off the cliff? We walk quickly for a while, and then
Tyler slows down till I'm beside him.

"I packed us a lunch," Tyler tells me. "Let's stop
up there." He points to a wooden deck overlooking
the cliff.

"I'm sorry about your mother," I tell him as we
settle on the bench.

"Thanks, but it was over five years ago." He takes
out two large plastic containers. The first one he
unsnaps has corn chips in it; the second is some
kind of dip.

"Oh my gawd. Is that what I think it is? Where
did you get hummus in this burg?"

He lifts his eyebrows and smiles. "I made it,
Zanna."

"For me?" I dip a chip and bite in. "Mmm, it's
amazing."

His smile broadens and he blushes. "It's not even hard. My mother's recipe. She was Greek."

I chew as I stare at him. Five years ago, he would have been twelve, a couple of years younger than Martin and I are now. Still, Martin and I have lived without one parent and each other since we were ten. In the sorry contest, we may have won.

"Have you ever been to Toronto?" I ask, because the silence has changed into that space from the edge of the cliff to the valley. If I don't say something, he's going to know I'm thinking about his mother's death.

"Yeah, for a couple of weeks once. My grand-parents live there and Mom took me to the Ex."

Our hands bump into each other dipping the chips. It's like a quick electric jolt up my arm, and I pull away. But the after-tingle is pleasant. I watch as his hand goes to dip again, see the faint blue veins beneath his tanned knuckles, the curve of his pointer finger as it meets his thumb. I'm staring really, and now his hand lifts the corn chip to his lips. They stretch into a smile. He knows I'm looking. I glance away, and at that moment Paris jumps up, planting his paws on the bench between us.

I throw a chip away from me and he happily snaps it up. I clear my throat. "So I bet you liked the rides—at the CNE, I mean."

Tyler takes a swig of water from his canteen, his Adam's apple bobbing as he swallows. "Nah, the ones at Canada's Wonderland are way better. What I liked best were the yachts at Ontario Place. I promised my mother we'd have one of those when I grew up."

"Not much use for a boat in the mountains." I look toward the white-and-blue peaks, sighing. "The mountains are beautiful though." Tyler nudges my hand with his canteen and I take it from him. Again our hands touch, but I can't pull away this time.

"Beautiful," he murmurs as he looks into my eyes. He smiles full-out now, and I feel myself leaning toward him. The air has a blue coolness to it like those mountains, but around my skin there's a warmer golden hum. "Do you miss Toronto?" he asks.

He's really asking about Zane, I can tell by his tone. I answer carefully. "I miss the subway. And the stores, all the choices. Plus, I never thought I'd say this: I miss the crowds. It's lonely out here."

He nods. We're so close I can feel his warm breath on my face. "I didn't want to come back from Toronto. My mother couldn't leave my father." It's a quiet admission of something—I'm not even sure quite what—but he sounds so sad.

I want to kiss him. He's sad and I'm lonely, and everything would feel better if our lips could just touch. I close my eyes and push my face forward.

But what about Zane? a tiny voice in the back of my head whispers. I back away for half a second and my eyes flutter open. Something knocks into my knees. I look down. It's Paris, of course, and he has something small and furry in his jaws. I draw back.

"What is that?"

The dog backs off the deck, shaking the creature in his mouth hard.

"Drop it, c'mon." I dash toward him, but he won't let go of whatever's in his mouth. He bows in front of me like it's a game. I feel a little sick. Whatever it is looks almost like a newborn kitten, but it has longer ears. "Tyler, help me. Paris is eating…a bunny."

Tyler's quicker than I am, grabbing Paris's head.

"Can you get him to let it loose?"

"It's too late."

"Leave it, leave it right now!" I grab Paris's muzzle and pinch it at the joint of his jaws so I force it open. The baby rabbit drops to the ground, making no attempt to break away.

"Zanna, he's snapped its neck. I have to…" Tyler steps forward hard on top of the animal. Paris runs back from a bush with another animal in his mouth. I scream at him. It's no use. Tyler's stomping that one to death now.

I head toward the shrub and see two tiny dark bodies lying underneath the greenery. When I move closer, I can't see any sign that the bunnies are alive.

Crying now, I step on each one of them too. Where is their mother?

I taste hummus backing up on me. Sneakers are one thing, soft furry babies are another. I kick dirt over the tiny bodies and swallow hard. I hate this place. I hate that dog. He runs around me happily, a greedy blood lust in his eyes. Like a satisfied vampire. Or maybe like a happy wolf. He tries to dig where the babies are and I push him away. "Get lost! Go away! Bad dog! Bad...wolf."

"He didn't do anything wrong. It's just his way." Tyler grabs Paris, dragging him from the burial site.

"Sorry," I whisper over the grave. I hear something ahead and see the mother rabbit springing away through the underbrush. "Where were you?" I yell after her, but she's far away before I can even finish. "How could you just desert them like that?" I shake my head. There's nothing more I can do for her babies either, so I head back onto the path. I can't look at Paris or at Tyler.

"Do you see?" Tyler asks. "Can you understand why the wolf retreat might be the best place for him?"

I can't answer. *If I'd left Paris there this morning, those bunnies would still be alive.*

Tyler packs up all of the lunch containers. Neither of us wants to eat anymore.

I swallow again, and we walk in silence back to the truck.

Paris jumps onto the front seat as usual. I push him back. I can't stand being around him. Tyler waits a while before turning the key.

In those few minutes, I decide. "You know what, Tyler? You're absolutely right. Let's turn around. It's not like I'll ever get Martin to agree anyway, and it's obvious that Paris belongs in the wolf retreat."

Chapter 10

Tyler's quiet as we drive. Quietly sure that he's right. I only wish I could be. Still, what exactly does a city girl know about wild animals? All I know is that I can't look at Paris. I hear and feel his hot panting across the back of my shoulder but I refuse to turn and see his tail wag for my approval. I don't want to start liking him again. He needs to stay in my mind as that creature with a bunny trapped in his fangs. That wolf with the shining, bloodthirsty eyes. Otherwise I won't be able to go through with it.

As we turn down the road toward the center, Paris jumps to the front and watches the road. I look to the side. When the truck pulls into the parking lot, I find myself stuck to the seat. "Tyler, can you just take Paris by yourself?"

Tyler scrunches his mouth up for a second. "Yes, if you're sure."

I nod, and he wrenches the door open.

Strangely, Paris doesn't leap out after him. Instead, he steps up onto my lap and licks my face. *The same tongue that lapped at a baby rabbit*, I tell myself but still I find myself scratching behind his ears. "You go on now. You're better off with your own kind." I push Paris toward the driver's side door.

He looks at me one more time, yellow eyes staring straight into mine. "Are you really sure?" they ask and, seeing no reprieve in mine, they finally turn away. After a moment, Paris leaps down and walks with Tyler toward the door.

They're gone a long time and it's warm, so I roll down the window. Dog sounds come again from behind the tall fence, yips and yaps. What really is the difference between a wolf and a dog? Then I hear it. One long howl, and I swear it's Paris's call. "It's for the best," I repeat, but my throat aches and I find it hard to swallow. Am I turning into Mom? Getting rid of someone just because he did something that bothered me?

Tyler returns. "You okay?"

"Fine. Let's go, though."

"Yeah, sure." He turns on the ignition and we roll. "Mind if we stop at the office? You can check your e-mail."

"That would be great," I answer and stare away to the side so he can't see my eyes. The trees, the rocks, the waterfalls: everything seems rougher and wilder as I see Paris again in my mind, dead baby rabbit in his mouth.

Yet already I feel as if something's opened up inside me and emptied. Something's missing as we roll into the lot in front of the Park Office. I don't have to push anyone back or sneak someone quietly past the front desk. It should all just be a huge relief.

"Hi," I call to Tyler's dad. I look down at the floor of the office. "Where's Quincy?"

"Hello." Tyler's dad smiles briefly. Then his mouth straightens. "Guess Tyler didn't tell you. I had to have Quincy put down yesterday."

"No. Um, I'm sorry." I keep walking. A feeling builds and rolls up through me. Surprisingly, not sadness or sympathy toward Tyler. Instead, it's a wave of anger. He never told me about Quincy. Why did he, the day after his dog was put down, show me the wolf retreat? Just because he lost his dog, does he have to make me lose mine too? *Give up, not lose,* I remind myself. I gave Paris up myself. It was really the best thing. I don't have to hide a big skulking wolf cub as I head for the computer at the back. I pass the stuffed wolf behind the plate-glass window. He's still eyeing the rabbit with a hard, yellow stare. Just like Paris.

I sit down at the keyboard and miss Paris chewing at my shoes. I quickly get to my mailer and download. Still nothing from Zane. I start a letter to him.

*Hey Zane. Maybe you're getting my e-mail but
I'm not getting yours. And it's so lonely out
here I actually miss Mom. I can't believe I just
wrote that.*

*I remember Tyler throwing the poppy over the
cliff. What if I had drowned in the river yesterday? How would Mom have felt? Bet she
would have felt sorry that she sent me off to
Dad's.*

*The dog we found under the cabin killed some
baby rabbits. Well, some of them I had to finish
for him, they were so far gone. I've never killed
anything before. Remember when I wouldn't let
you step on that daddy long legs? You thought
I was so goofy for picking it up in a tissue and
setting it free outside. So maybe Tyler, the
ranger dude, was right. The dog is a wolf.
That's what I think at least, so I had him com-
mitted to a wolf retreat. I wish I knew whether
I did the right thing.*

*Mostly it's beautiful out here but it's also
empty, untouched, wild...and just lonely. I
could take it if you were here, or Mom. Please
write. Love Zanna.*

I press *Send* and then look at the list of e-mails
from Mom. *Love You, Paris News, Exciting News,*

*More Exciting News, Call Me, Answer Quickly, Last
Chance.* I decide to click on the last one first. Maybe
the subject header means she's visiting soon.

> *Zanna, my love. I need to book the plane tick-
> ets by 6 a.m. Friday, your time. I've tried to
> call your Dad's satellite phone, but knowing
> him, he's switched it off till he's in the moun-
> tains. Call me immediately.*

There's a string of numbers that doesn't resemble
any phone number in Canada but I look at my watch
and I feel sick. It's 4:00 p.m. Too late. Maybe she
can't come now. I click on *Answer Quickly.*

> *Darling Zanna, You must still be very angry at
> me, but don't let your feelings get in the way of
> the experience of a lifetime. Let me know if
> Dad can get you to Calgary Airport by Sunday
> and I'll get the plane tickets for you.*

Plane tickets for me? She hadn't been planning
a visit. Plane tickets for where? I wonder, as I click
open *Call Me.* You never knew with Mom. If there was
a big time limit, maybe I was supposed to meet her
somewhere: Rome, London, New York City. I breathe
a little quicker imagining it all.

Hey Zanna, Call me. The seat sale is almost over. Don't miss out!

I open *More Exciting News.*

Monsieur Langois has just made the most generous offer. He has a travel budget for the featured artist but since I am already in residence, he will fly a family member in for my show. You're the only one who appreciates art. Isn't it wonderful? Write back soon so I can make all the arrangements.

She doesn't want me to live with her after all. "A visit is better than not seeing Paris at all," I tell the screen and copy the long string of numbers down. I run to the front. "Please can I use your phone? I need to call my mother right now. It's long distance but my dad can pay you back. I'm going to Paris!"

Tyler's dad smiles as he hands me a receiver. I key in all the digits slowly to get it right; still, the ring doesn't even sound the same, and I'm sure I must have done it wrong when someone finally picks up. "*Oui, allô?*" It's a man's voice.

I would hang up, especially since he sounds hesitant, sleepy maybe, but I hear my mother's voice in the background. "*Ma mère,*" I say in my best school

French. "*Je cherche Joanna Segal qui est ma mère.*"

I hear background noise, crackling. "What's wrong, Zanna?" Mom asks me in a breathless rush.

"What's wrong? I thought you invited me to your Paris show. I'm calling you back like you asked."

"But the deadline was this morning. It's past midnight here. You're sure everyone's all right?"

"Yes. What do you mean about the deadline?"

She pauses on the other end. I hear crackling. "The seat sale. It's over. Did you not read my e-mails? I can't ask Jacques to pay the full fare for you."

"But what about the travel budget they have for you? Dad can pay the difference. Or I could use the money in my account."

"Zanna, the difference would be over a thousand dollars."

"Okay, well then Dad can drive me to Calgary on Sunday and I can go standby. That will be cheap too, right?"

"I don't think so, Zanna."

"It's the experience of a lifetime, like you said, Mom. Dad and I can make it work." I hear the rumble of Jacques' voice in the background but can't hear or understand what he's saying.

"Zanna, when you didn't call in time, I took it as a sign and made a decision. We're supposed to be apart for a while. We both need the space."

I inhale deeply and let the air out. "Because of Jacques," I whisper to her.

"Honey, he's the one who originally suggested you come, so don't be mad at him. But I have to have a life too."

"Mom, he's answering your phone after midnight. I already know you're sleeping with him."

"Oh, grow up!" she snaps. "I know you check your e-mail obsessively. If I'd been that boy, you'd have answered me immediately." She catches herself and stops. Dead silence. Thousands of miles away, across an ocean, Mom sighs. "There you go. Do you see what I mean? You know how to push all my buttons."

I swallow hard, willing myself not to beg and not to cry.

"Are you there, Zanna?"

Another swallow and then I make myself tough.

"Where else would I be?"

"Don't be that way. I'm the one who won't have anyone from my family to see my exhibit."

"That's right." I swallow hard, realizing all she wanted was an audience. She didn't really miss me at all. "Mom, I have to go. Someone else needs to use the phone. Bye." I slam down the receiver to cut off her answer.

"Easy," Mr. Benson says. "I know you're excited

about your trip, but I might want to call someone else
another time."

"There is no trip," I whisper; it's all I can manage.
I feel like throwing my head back and howling. Instead,
I walk back to the Internet computer. Slumping back
into the chair, I have to sign on again because the
computer has timed me out. Just like Mom.

I go back to the list of e-mails from Mom and tap
Enter to read the one with the subject header
Exciting News.

*Zanna, I'm so excited and so frustrated at the
same time. You're not around to hear my good
news. I'm to be feature artist at the Galerie
Jacques, starting this weekend. I wish you
could be here for the opening. You who have
always been around through all my struggles.*

Her good news, her art show, her struggles. It's
always about her. The fact that she's not around for
me just isn't something she ever considers. I open
Paris News next.

*Hi Zanna, I'm painting the cliché Paris scenes.
For me, they are all beautiful: the Eiffel Tower,
the café on the corner, the Arc de Triomphe. I
suppose I should e-mail you some photographs*

*so you can see for yourself. I feel so happy
here. So free. I love it.*

Of course she feels free: she doesn't have me. I rub
at my eyes. One more to read, then I'm all caught up.

*Love You. The flat is small, gray, and dingy.
The bathroom has the ugliest stained tub and
there's only one bedroom. I know how you like
your privacy so I'm sure I made the right decision. You wouldn't have been happy here.*

Yeah right, I think. There you go. Only one bedroom, and Mom and Jacques want their privacy. Me
on the couch would just not have cut it. That was
the big decision she made when I didn't call by her
stupid deadline.

*I know you'll love the mountains and being
with your father and brother much better. Still,
I miss you darling. I love you xxxooooo, Mom.*

Okay, so I'm going to suck it up and write her
back. I want to act nonchalant like I really don't
care. I want to be mature and congratulate her on
her success so she'll regret not having me at her
show. So she'll miss the *me* that used to get along

with her, the one who was her best friend. Instead, every bad thought comes out through my fingertips.

Hey Mom. You're still a mother with two children, so how dare you act like you're a free spirit and do whatever you like?
And c'mon, I'm so far from civilization, phones, and the Internet, I can't return your e-mails zip-zap. Let's face it: you planned it that way so I couldn't connect with Zane. As far as privacy goes, I'm sharing a room with Martin. Only a curtain separates us. A couch in your living room sounds like luxury. You're painting Paris scenes and yes, I have beautiful mountains. Still, I can't even get canvas to paint anything on. So much for your parting present. And all this would be okay, really, it would be, if I could only believe you loved me. Because if you really loved and missed me, it wouldn't have mattered about the extra thousand dollars my ticket would cost. Or the strawberry tattoo on my ankle. Or the boys I like that you can't stand. You know in the end you just sold me down the line. You wanted your boyfriend Jacques as your audience right now, not me.

I stop. Letting all my feelings out isn't helping.

The thing is, once you write something, it's there on the screen in front of you, black and white, true and hard, something to face. And I can't face it all right now. I place the cursor at the end of the message and backspace, watching the jittery cursor make my problems disappear.

CHAPTER 11

WHEN TYLER COMES TO THE BACK TO GET ME, HE KNOWS something's up but he doesn't say anything. He just watches me. I try not to show anything. We climb into the truck.

He sticks the key in the ignition but doesn't turn it. "Now that we're alone, do you want to talk about whatever went on back there?" Tyler finally asks. "One moment you're wildly excited and going to Paris. Next moment you're...this?" He gestures with both hands toward me.

My arms are folded and I'm hunched over. I kick out at the hump dividing our sides of the truck.

He's facing me, blue eyes unblinking, expecting me to open up and share.

I want to kick him. "Why didn't you tell me about Quincy?" I stare out the side window at the crappy house across the street where the old woman with the walker lives.

"C'mon, Zanna, why should I have?" he says gently. I don't turn back to him; instead, I kick the door.

"Quincy was Dad's dog, and it's not like you even

knew him." The engine roars up in agreement. I feel his hand on my shoulder. "Why should I make you sad about him?"

"Do you feel bad about him being put down?" I turn back to look at him, wanting to know that someone feels as awful as I do.

"What do you think?"

He's watching the road now, staring straight ahead, but I hear it in his voice. There's a hole inside him too, so I decide to tell him about Mom. "Okay. It has nothing to do with Quincy and nothing to do with Paris. Or at least not the dog Paris. My mother changed her mind about my trip to France."

"What?" Tyler brakes hard for a bump in the road. We still bounce up and down. "Why?"

"She says it's because I missed a seat sale. I didn't answer her e-mails in time and I never called back before the closing date."

Tyler's brow furrows and the truck speeds up again. "You still having trouble with the computer? I swear no one else does."

"You're right, only me. I'm the only one who doesn't open e-mails that say *Answer Quickly* and *Last Chance*."

"Oh, ohhh!" His mouth buckles with sympathy. "Maybe you should give her the Park Office number for next time."

I raise an eyebrow at him but he's driving around a pothole and concentrating.

"There'll be other seat sales, right?"

I shake my head. "Maybe after she dumps the boyfriend living with her." I swallow hard. "Honestly, I think my mother wants me to live with Dad so she can just do anything she wants."

"C'mon, you're not a little kid. They're not married anymore. She can date whomever she wants." I kick the divider hump again. "They never were married," I say quietly.

"Yes, well, they're also separated, obviously."

"Physically, like in different countries. But they've never really explained what's going on to me and Martin. They just do their own thing. They divided Martin and me up because they thought we should live with the parent of the same sex. They never asked us what we wanted. I missed my brother!"

"That's rough." Tyler grips the steering wheel, staring straight ahead, no judgment in his voice. "So how do you know she's living with a guy?"

"He answered the phone and it's past midnight over there."

"There could be lots of other explanations."

"Nah. She dated in Toronto too, but just snuck around. Thought I was stupid. My boyfriend is supposed to be the reason for shipping me off to the hinterland. Clearly it's her wanting to have one that's the real factor."

"Hard to take, isn't it?" Tyler glances toward me and then back at the road. "I mean, that your parents can't be perfect. The Father's Day and Mother's Day cards all make out like everyone else's parents are."

Mother's Day cards. He's got that right; they're the worst. *You're always there for me. You understand when no one else can. You make me feel special.* I mean, none of those apply. I knuckle at my eyes trying to force the tears to stay inside. I will not let my mother make me cry.

I take a deep breath and put my hands down again, watching Tyler's profile. He's got a lot of wrinkles around his eyes for a seventeen-year-old. I never noticed that before. They make him look older. His mother died; maybe sadness makes him more mature. Still, he didn't sound sad about his mom as much as disappointed.

We turn onto the dirt road to the cabin. He starts on another topic. "What are you going to say to Martin?"

"Um, um...I don't know." We roll into the driveway of our cabin and I realize I can't face my brother. He wasn't there for the rabbit massacre: how can I expect him to understand? "Tyler, can you stay a while? Just till the crew all gets back,"

"Can't do it alone, eh?"

I shake my head.

He shrugs his shoulder. "Sure. Just wish you had a phone so I could call home and let Joyce know I'll be late for supper."

"Don't we all." I roll my eyes. "Can I get you some orange juice?"

"A glass of water would be fine."

We walk into the cabin together; it's unlocked, the joy of living in the country. I get us a couple of glasses of water but then it seems claustrophobic in the living room, the air sticky. "Can we go onto the deck?" I stand in front of the sliding door, glasses in hand.

He slides the door back and we sit staring at the lake. It's choppy, a moody gray, with the mountains in the background, dark charcoal. Plum-colored clouds gather on the skyline. I shiver. "Looks like a storm's coming."

"Yeah, the wind's picking up. Guess your dad will be home soon, then." Tyler looks back toward the road, as if expecting him.

"I don't know. Remember, he camps out in Arctic blizzards." I shiver again at the thought. What if he does decide to stay out all night? Without Martin or Paris, I'll be all alone in a shack in the mountains. It's not like I could ask Tyler to stay the night.

"You're cold; do you want to go inside?" Tyler asks.

"No, really, I'm fine." I shudder again. Mom had a cow when she came home once and Zane and I were alone in the apartment, doing absolutely nothing. I don't know Dad's rules. Maybe he'd do the same, or he'd have a moose instead.

"At least go and get a jacket," Tyler says. "I'd give you mine but I left my backpack in the truck."

I dash back in and grab one of Dad's from the closet. It's heavy, with a quilt lining, and it drapes down to below my knees.

"There you go! Better?"

I nod and stare out at the lake. My hands on the arms of the chair are almost covered by the sleeves. Tyler puts his hand on top of mine and it feels good, warm, reassuring...and maybe something else.

I love Zane; my mother's wrong about separating us and expecting it to end. Besides, Tyler isn't holding my hand boyfriend/girlfriend style. It's more like a friendship thing. But the warmth of his hand makes me stop shivering, and it makes me feel other things besides bad. I stare at his lips and wonder what a kiss from him would be like.

I'm really glad when I hear the ATV lumbering up behind the house a couple of minutes later. Glad, relieved, but maybe deep down just a tiny bit disappointed.

Following our larger ATV, one of the smaller quads rolls up with Cassandra and Jason. Dad and Drew climb down from the larger one.

Something prickles at the back of my neck. "I don't see Martin anywhere. Where's Martin?"

"You've got three ATVs, right? He must have fallen behind." Tyler shades his eyes with a hand as though that will help him see. He squints and strains his neck.

That must be it. Martin would have begged and pleaded to ride a quad all by himself. He must be thrilled that he got the chance.

Dad stomps up the stairs to the deck. "Hey guys. Have a good day?"

"Um, not exactly." I stare at him hard for a second. "Dad have you switched your satellite phone on lately?"

"Geez, no. Forgot. Costs so much per minute, I rarely do."

"Maybe you should check your messages now. Mom invited me to Paris."

He takes out his oversize phone and punches in some numbers. "She did? But you just got here." His eyebrows and shoulders shrug in unison as he hears my mother's message. "Why would you drive all this way just to turn around and fly for six hours?" He pauses. "Apparently your mom sent you e-mails too."

"I didn't open them in time."

He shrugged his shoulders again. "Like I said, why would you want to go to Paris now?"

"Da-ad? Are you crazy? Paris is a world-class city. I'd kill to go there."

"Oh? Just thought you two had had enough of each other. Where's Martin?"

Now the strange sensation tingles right up my spine. "Wait a minute, Martin's with you, isn't he?" Suddenly I can't breathe. I remember the icy needles of water in my mouth and up my nose when I fell into the water yesterday. Why am I feeling that now? What does it mean?

"Why would Martin be with me? You heard me tell him he has to volunteer this summer with you." Dad slides back the patio door and hollers in. "Martin?"

"Dad, he didn't go with us this morning. Martin definitely told me he was going off with you guys." *He's not in there*, I want to tell Dad. I know because I can feel it clearly now. Martin's missing. Martin's in trouble.

"Martin! Martin?" Dad enters the cabin and climbs the stairs to the loft. No Martin there, obviously, so he pounds back down.

The cabin's not big enough for him to search long. A quick glance in the kitchen and bedroom, and then he's back outside. "That's funny. Where could he be?"

"Hey Cassie!" Dad calls across the field between the cabins. She's standing on her deck, the wind tossing her hair as she clunks her work boots together, knocking off some dirt.

"Yeah?"

"Have any of you seen Martin?"

I can see her shaking her head, but she ducks back into the crew cabin. After a minute, she comes back. "Nobody saw him all day."

She unties her long, albino-white ponytail and reties it as she heads down behind the cabins where all the vehicles are parked.

"And where's that dog? He's got to be wherever Martin is." Dad looks around the house as though expecting to spot Paris.

"I turned Paris over to the Rocky Mountain Wolf Haven."

"You what!" Dad sputters.

"Sir, it was my idea. The dog is a wolf, and we thought he'd—"

Cassandra interrupts, breathless, at the foot of the stairs to the deck. "Doc, the quad with the carburetor problems is missing. Do you think Martin went for a joyride?"

Dad shakes his head. "He wouldn't have the keys."

"Um, yes, he actually might." Cassandra blushes. "They were in the ignition." She holds up her hands as if to ward off blame. "I know what you're thinking but half the time the thing doesn't start. And it's annoying to always carry the extra set around. This was just easier."

"He got that quad running—trust me, I know," I tell them. Even back when Martin was nine, he loved engines.

"Actually, Drew suggested Martin have a go at taking the engine apart yesterday."

"All right. Let's assume he took the ATV out for a spin. Where should we look?" Dad's eyes sharpen, brightening, hardening. He doesn't look scared so I decide I don't need to be either.

My brain sharpens too, as I think back to this morning when Martin whispered and shushed me. Why had he been so secretive? He didn't want Dad to know, of course. "Dad, Martin followed you guys out this morning. Only he hung back so you wouldn't see him."

"What? But why?" Dad lifts up his hands as though wanting me to put the answer into them.

I can't look at Dad's eyes. The accusation burns hot across my face. "Martin wanted to find out whether you're working for Skylon."

CHAPTER 12

DAD SAYS NOTHING FOR A SECOND. I HATE THE SILENCE. I want Dad to tell me that he's only up in these mountains to study the glaciers and measure ice depth or density, that they all provide the clue to understanding our future climatology—that Martin's crazy and he would never work for Skylon. But Dad doesn't. Is he lost in thought about where Martin could be, or is he guilty of selling out? "Drew, Jason!" he shouts suddenly. "Get over here. We've got to go out again and look for my son."

My son. Dad's voice wobbles a bit on the words, and that wobble confirms that he's seriously worried about Martin. Skylon seems an issue he doesn't even consider at this time.

Drew and Jason rush over, Jason eating from a tin of spaghetti. A red noodle-y dinosaur shape clings to his mustache. He wipes at it with the back of his sleeve.

Dad explains again what I said. "Did anyone notice another ATV behind us this morning?" he asks in an exasperated voice.

Drew scratches his head where his hair should be growing. "You can't really hear anything over the noise of the engines."

"Did you ever look back?"

Drew shakes his head.

"What about you, Jason? You were in the rear car."

"Yeah..." Jason hesitates, his face sagging into a kind of punched-in look of discouragement. "No, really not once. Sorry, Doc."

"You, Cassie?" Dad asks.

"Mmm, I don't know. When we were driving along the ridge over the river, just a little after the path meets the road, I thought I caught a glimpse of red through some trees."

The ATV is red.

"So that's where we'll look first."

"Sir?" Tyler starts. "May I make a suggestion?"

"What?" Dad snaps.

"Call in the Skylon helicopter. It's going to be dark in another couple of hours, and," he looks up at the sky, "it may storm even sooner."

Dad pulls out his large phone and immediately punches in the numbers.

If Dad doesn't work for Skylon, why would he have their phone number?

"I should call my father too," Tyler says, wincing. "He'll want to organize a search-and-rescue team fast."

Cassandra sucks in a breath and covers her mouth.

"Just in case," Tyler rushes to explain. "It's such a large area and the temperature's dropping. Better to get going quickly."

Dad sticks a finger in his non-phone ear.

"When?" he shouts at the person on the other end of the line. "All right. We'll call you if something changes. Otherwise, sunrise at the airport." He hands the phone to Tyler.

Tyler gets his father right away, but it's clear by the side of the conversation I can hear that no search party can be sent out tonight. Before he can hand back the phone, a sudden rush of rain sends us into the house. Once the patio door shuts, the rain sounds like distant applause.

"Wish Quincy was still around," Tyler says. "I'd head out with him right away, even if it was storming."

"Well, I'm going out right now," Dad says. "This is ridiculous—we could all be worried over nothing. Martin could be tinkering with the engine somewhere not two kilometers from here. You know how he loses all sense of time when his hands are on a motor."

Sure, in the rain, I think. "I'm going with you," I tell him. Somehow that will make up for me giving away Martin's pet. And for not wanting to live up

here and share a room with my brother. Or for sim-
ply deserting Martin this morning and leaving him
to his own stupid plans, which, somewhere deep
down inside, I'm convinced I knew about. I mean,
why did he shush me when I asked him about going
out with Dad?

"No, you stay here in case he gets back." Dad's
already stomping down the stairs outside, the rain
plastering down his hair. But I follow close behind,
the hood of the jacket I borrowed over my own head.

"I have to come."

"I can stay in the cabin and wait, Doc," Cassandra volunteers. "I'll use the walkie-talkie if he
shows up."

"Dad, please. I think. wherever he is, I may be
able to sense his presence. You know, that twin
thing we've got going."

Dad shrugs, then nods.

"I'd like to help too. The more eyes the better,"
Tyler says, and we all head up toward the larger yellow ATV. It's got six-wheel drive and tractor treads
for the snow. We're hurrying, and without warning
my right foot slides in the fresh mud. Splat.
I land butt-down in it.

"You okay?" Tyler reaches a hand toward me and
I grab it.

"Fine, just mucky." I don't even brush any of it

off, just scramble up and try to dig in the edges of my boots. The larger ATV seats four, has a space for equipment in the back, and, luckily with today's weather, has a roof and snap-down plastic windows. Tyler and I climb in the back; Dad's the chauffeur.

The engine rumbles and the ATV moves forward, riding like a tractor, bumpy but sure. We drive along the road first. Both sides are lined with tall fir trees; there's no way Martin could have driven off the path here without leaving some broken branches behind as evidence. Still, my eyes shift back and forth, looking for any glimpse of color between the boughs: the red ATV, or some article of clothing of Martin's. Nothing. I feel empty.

"I don't like this rain," Tyler says. "It's so dark, I'm not sure we'll be able to spot him."

I narrow my eyes and scan the landscape constantly, never blinking. We ride for ten minutes like that, and my head feels like it's rattling and rumbling along with the ATV. At a small wooden sign that reads *Ribbon Glacier Trail*, we turn off. The ride becomes bumpier and mud splatters up all around us. The ATV climbs now, a little slower, the engine seeming even noisier. Up, up. The path clings to the edge over a river where the water rushes even louder than the engine.

"Wish your dad would drive a little slower," Tyler

tells me, as he looks toward the sound of the water nervously.

"How much slower can he go?" I shout at him.

"Huh, what?" Dad turns and jabs his finger at the leftside of the road. "I think this is where Cassie said she might have seen him."

We all stare to that side but the trees have turned into a blur of shadow behind a tissue-paper mist, the rain fogging everything beyond a few feet.

Suddenly the ATV comes to a complete halt. Dad opens the glove compartment and takes a map out from under what looks like a bunch of red candles, or maybe dynamite.

Tyler shakes his head at the blinding rain. "Do you keep emergency flares in the other ATV too?"

"Not in the one with the carburetor difficulty. We weren't intending to use that one until it got repaired." Dad unfolds the map and squints at it.

"Do you think Martin packed some warm gear? Or some food?"

"It was warm this morning." I shrug my shoulders. "He'd have brought himself a few granola bars for sure. Yeah, I think he would have even packed a sandwich since he wouldn't have expected Dad to bring him anything."

"Why don't we get out and have a look?" Tyler says as he slides out the side. I follow him, and Dad jumps out too. A small ditch is forming on the side of the path, filling with water, but I step over it.

Tyler scans the ground as he walks. "I don't see any ATV tracks. Is there any point to going further in this?" He holds up his hands to catch the rain.

"I want to," I say. I try to think like Martin, feel like him. I close my eyes but I still get nothing.

Dad looks at a small black box—his Global Positioning System—and shakes his head. "I can't pick up any satellites in this weather. We can't go far, Zanna, or we'll get lost ourselves."

"No more than five minutes," Tyler says. Then he removes a whistle from his pocket and blows it three times, pausing for a moment between blasts.

"Just in case he's lost nearby, maybe he'll hear us," he explains as we all head through the trees.

The leaves and branches block the rain for a while, and I find myself secretly hoping Martin's found someplace dry. He's smart that way. He could have built himself a shelter—he's great with a hammer. I smile, remembering the tree fort he built with me back before he left. We both fell out, breaking opposite arms. Mom was so steamed.

'Course, Martin doesn't have a hammer today. Still, that wouldn't stop him. I can picture some kind of lean-to, perhaps made with branches and logs. I shake that image—it's not coming in clearly, so it can't be real. Martin must be somewhere dry though, and I find myself scanning for any kind of shelter.

Only, where's the ATV? I squint. We should be able to spot it somewhere.

Tyler whistles again.

I spot a flash of red to my left and run, trying to push away the mist with my arms. Darn. A red plastic flag on a tree, a trail marker. Another pinpoint of red turns out to be a bottle cap. Oh great, now I find garbage! A larger patch of red to the right catches my eye and I head for it, but that turns out to be the leaves of a burned-out old bush.

I turn around and don't see Tyler or Dad anymore. They've vaporized into white air. "Hey!" I call out. "Where are you guys?"

A whistle blows and I walk toward it. Which direction was that from? It's easy to get confused in all this rain and mist. The whistle blows again. How far did I walk? The whistle sounds closer now, and I bump into Tyler.

"Where'd you go?" Tyler asks. "This is crazy. I couldn't even see you. We've got to turn around and head back."

But I spot some more red. "Over there!" I point, and we run together—to yet another patch of leaves.

"You're right, there's no use." Tyler grabs my forearm and leads me toward Dad.

We scramble back to the path. "You're sure Cassie meant in the trees? She couldn't have seen him along the riverbank?"

We look toward where we can hear the water, but now there's only white mist. We can't see anything, but I remember that it's a long way down. Martin might have slid over to that side of the trail. He might have fallen over. I feel the icy needles in my mouth again and a choking sensation. No, no, it can't be. Martin's just broken down somewhere, that's all: positive thinking, positive thinking. He's not hurt or...I can't even finish that thought.

Tyler whistles another time and we stand waiting silently, desperately, hopelessly. Dad gazes up at the washed-out sky; his lips are buttoned around things he won't say. He shakes his head. Finally we climb back into the ATV.

Dad keeps driving. I don't know why, because it's impossible to see anything.

"Sir, unless the engine quit right here on the trail, we aren't going to find Martin tonight." Tyler has to shout over the roar of the engine and the rush of rain.

"Well, what if it did?" Dad shouts back.

"Wouldn't you have seen him on the way back?"

"Not if he broke down on the way home."

It makes no sense, I think. Martin really just

wanted to spy on Dad to make sure he was doing his usual drilling and snow-measuring. Would he really have hung around the whole day, hidden, just in case someone from Skylon showed up for a secret meeting? His spying made no sense either. It isn't like you can eavesdrop on a conversation that's taking place in an ATV. What could he have hoped to find out today?

The rushing becomes louder and the ATV climbs up and up. In the mist ahead, I can make out a waterfall that looks as high as the CN Tower.

"Ribbon Falls," Tyler tells me. "In the sunlight, it's quite spectacular."

We don't stop to admire it, and I squint my eyes, hoping to see Martin. My head aches and my eyes feel tight from scrunching. When we reach the top, we drive along a cliff that hangs over the lake. At least with the drop, we know he can't be broken down on that side. My breath catches.

After another hour, we're at the toe of Ribbon Glacier. Dad stops. I can make out the huge white swirl of ice and snow that circles two peaks, which, if you could see it properly, probably would appear to be something like a white ribbon. Dad is breathing hard as he steps out, as though he's trying to calm himself down. Not a good sign. Tyler and I step out too. The rain hits hard here. It's colder and blobs on us, half snow, half water.

Dad stands with his hands on his hips, a frown on his face, and a stream of water dripping off his nose. He shakes his head. I sneeze, and Dad turns. "Let's get back in. I'm just going to check the shack and then we'll head back."

The ATV rolls onto the snow, and Dad aims it toward a little white hut. He parks alongside it and jumps out.

"Why would he be in there?" I ask after he leaves. "I mean, the other ATV's nowhere in sight."

"Your dad's just reaching here. Give him a break. We're this close and you never know, maybe Martin broke down and walked here instead of back."

A shelter—sure, Martin might have done that.

"Oh, I just want to kill him for taking off like this."

Tyler just stares at me, his mouth straight.

"Don't look like that. He's going to be okay. I know nothing could have happened to him. Why the heck he went off the trail is beyond me."

"Well, if he really wanted to follow your dad without being seen, it makes sense, doesn't it? And just because your father didn't see him, doesn't mean that wherever your dad was driving, Martin couldn't see him."

Dad runs back from the hut. No luck, obviously. We drive home with the headlights of the ATV lighting up the fog eerily. I'm starving, cold, and exhausted. I bury my head in my hands.

"Don't worry. He'll be fine for one night," Tyler tells me in an even, measured tone. "And tomorrow when the weather clears, we should have no problem finding him with the helicopter."

I lift my head. "But what if it doesn't clear?"

CHAPTER 13

I CAN HEAR DAD PACING ALL NIGHT LONG. HE'S WAITING UP, I think. Hoping the rain will stop and praying that Martin will return. Only neither happens.

The next morning, the helicopter can't fly. It's still raining hard. White fog hides everything beyond arm's length and the search party can't hunt for Martin either.

Tyler's still at our cabin. He stayed the night, thinking he'd be out with the first search party. Dad put out a sleeping bag on the pullout couch in the living room.

I stare out at the rain through the tiny window in the kitchen. Tyler's chowing down on the breakfast Dad's fried up for him, and the bacon-and-eggs smell makes me check down at my feet for Paris. Of course he's not nosing around down there: he's back at the Rocky Mountain Wolf Haven.

"I wish I hadn't given Paris up. It feels like the moment I abandoned the dog, my brother disappeared. Sort of like they're psychically linked somehow." I turn my spoon around in my yogurt. "Hey, what about a dog?" I ask Tyler. "You said if you had Quincy, you'd go out no matter what. There must be other search-and-rescue animals."

"Quincy was the only one in the area. And there's been an earthquake in San Salvador. I happen to know the other SAR teams are down there." Tyler sips at his orange juice. Suddenly his eyebrows lift and he gulps. "What did you just say about Paris?"

"I said I wish we hadn't—"

"That's it!" He snaps his finger at me. "Let's get Paris back. Only a dog can find someone in this storm."

"You said he was a wolf."

"Even better. More in touch with his nose. Look, it's a really long shot, I know. We train search-and-rescue dogs for hours every week, and Paris is pretty wild. He may chase the scent of a bear over your brother. But it's worth a try. I'll call the center on your dad's phone."

Tyler dials, and I listen to his side of the conversation with Peter Kerrigan at the wolf center. The question is, of course, how to get Paris back inside. Normally Peter feeds the wolves on Friday, so they naturally come to the building. But today is Saturday and they're all reasonably full. He's going to throw out another deer carcass: their sense of smell is strong, and they're greedy...still.

Tyler hangs up and we take off to the truck. He drives pretty fast through the rain and mist. "If only it would stop." He shakes his head. He sounds as impatient as I feel. We still can't see anything and Tyler misses the turnoff. As he backs up the truck, he misjudges the edge of the road and the truck slides into the ditch, the front end still clinging to the road. "Damn."

A rumbling from behind us signals another vehicle's approach. It's a car, barreling out of the mist, heading straight for the truck. Can it stop in time?

"Hold on!" Tyler reverses hard, and we bump down off the road backward. The car passes, the driver leaning on the horn the whole time.

Tyler mutters something back, then throws the gearshift into first and we plow down, and up onto the road again.

The retreat's only another couple of kilometers away. We park and walk to the observation room. "I was expecting my caribou shipment Monday. Afraid the wolves will just have to satisfy themselves with my personal supply of ground beef and cube steak." Tyler and Peter scatter the meat out back. "Their sense of smell is a million times better than ours, so this should bring them in."

When they're finished, they step back inside. "If this doesn't work, we could try again on Monday."

Sylvia McNicoll

Monday. How long can a person last in the cold without food or water? Peter and Tyler sit down beside me on the bench facing the one-way glass window.

I turn to Peter. "Now what?"

"Now we wait. They may not come at all. I always warn the visitors. Even with a fresh kill in the yard, there's no guarantee."

We sit and watch. Soon enough Konan, the black wolf, approaches furtively followed by Chinook, the white one. Wolf by wolf, they show up and snatch mouthfuls of steak.

I look them all over and shake my head. "Paris isn't out there."

Konan snaps and nips at Chinook right in front of me. Only a window pane separates us. Peter frowns.

"Shouldn't Paris be out there with them? Why isn't he?"

"They may have killed him on the spot."

"What? Why would you let me put my dog in there, then?"

"Because a wolf doesn't stand a chance otherwise. I saw it happen when I was in school, so I know. A bunch of us started slipping some wolves food on a regular basis. Right from our hand—not like here, where they don't even know we're behind the glass. They lost their fear of humans and expected food from them. Raided campgrounds. In the end, the head ranger made us go out and shoot them. Said we were responsible. I never felt so bad in my life. And I never forgot it. This was your wolf's best chance at a life."

"I'm going to call him."

"If you go out there, you'll just scatter them."

"Good. I don't want all the wolves, just Paris." I push open the door slightly and call, "Paris, Paris!" For a moment, Konan looks up from his meal, staring me directly in the eyes.

Peter steps forward, rifle in hand.

"I thought you said they'd scatter," I hiss at him. He lifts the rifle to his shoulder. "They're wild animals. Unpredictable." Chinook lopes off. Peter swivels and aims the rifle at Konan now. "Don't worry, it's only a tranquilizer gun," he tells me. Konan skulks off after Chinook. The other wolves head back into the woods too.

"Paris?" I put two fingers between my lips and whistle long and hard. "Paris! You better come right now!" With the wolves gone from the yard, I step out the door and alternate calling and whistling.

Then I see Paris, or at least a wolf that resembles him. Same black and brown markings, same heart-shaped white mask around the eyes. Only he skulks out of the bush, his yellow eyes even more intense. From his throat to his shoulder is an ugly red gash. It *is* Paris.

"Oh, Paris. Come here, boy. I'm so sorry."

For a moment, Paris's yellow eyes stare into mine. Does he hate me? But his tail wags in slow recognition. He whimpers and runs to me. I throw my arms around his neck and hug him.

"No time for that. Get in!" Peter yells at me.

I grab the scruff of Paris's neck, gently so as not to hurt his wound, and guide him in through the door. Peter slams it after us.

"Look who was coming back for your pet!" He points to Konan, who's running straight for the door. Peter turns to face me. "Close call." He leans against the door and seems to be catching his breath.

"Look,"I say, I'm sorry for all the trouble I caused. I made a mistake. Paris likes people too much and he's a puppy. He obviously can't hold his own out there with the likes of Konan or even Chinook." I run my hand gingerly along the gash near his neck.

"Trouble? That's all yet to come. A wolf does not make a good pet. And if he finds your brother, it'll be a miracle."

He has to be wrong. My arms circle Paris's neck, and he licks my face from chin to forehead, across my mouth and nose. I smile and don't even care what his mouth had in it before or what that tongue has touched. "I'll pay you back for all that meat you threw out for the wolves." I want to leave quickly, escape his critical stare and look for Martin.

Peter holds up his hands. "Never mind. You can sign up as a Friend of the Haven sometime. Learn to appreciate wolves from the proper distance."

I promise to come back and do that when we have more time and I have my allowance in my pocket. We rush through the wolf displays toward the exit. I feel better already with Paris back at my feet, and as I step from the building it's as if we're stepping into a whole new world of bright, white sunshine. "Look at that. It's clearing up! The search party will be able to go out."

"You're right. We better hurry." Tyler's words are terse, his mouth tight.

Paris and I run to the truck with him. A lone howl makes Paris stop for a moment, his ears up.

"Never mind them, boy. You have a new family now."

Paris opens his long snout into a grin that drops into a pant. Then he wags his tail and scrambles into the truck with me.

I don't mind on the way back when Paris stands on me, his long claws digging into my jeans, his thick. furry tail brushing over my face.

"Easy," I tell Tyler as the truck spins around the turn, throwing Paris and me against him. "You don't want to put us in the ditch again."

Tyler's hands grip the steering wheel, his mouth as tight as his knuckles.

"What's the matter?"

"If the search party beats us there, they'll walk all over the scents and ruin it for Paris. It's tough enough for a trained SAR dog, but for Paris..."

"Is there a shortcut we can take to get us close to the trail?" I ask.

"Right, sure there is." Tyler brightens. At the next adjoining dirt road he turns off, and when he comes to the first trail, parks the truck.

"Sky Mountain Trail?"

"That's right. Are you up for a little reverse climbing?"

Chapter 14

Tyler grabs some flares from his glove compartment and shoves them in the backpack. "Ready?"

I nod.

"Then let's do it!" He breaks into a jog and Paris leaps ahead of him. No time for scenery observation, and there's still a layer of mist anyway; we tear over the whole trail that we covered yesterday, past the unmarked graves of the rabbit babies. I'm over that now, I tell myself, as I swallow hard.

Paris doesn't even pause. He loves to run and he seems to sense the urgency of the cause. We finally stop at the cliff where the blue poppies grow. I hang, doubled over, breathing hard, in and out, waiting to catch my breath.

Tyler stands near the edge, silent, in that unreachable place he was at yesterday. His mother died here, and here is where we're beginning our search for Martin: an ending and a beginning. What can he be thinking? He seems to sway as he stares ahead. Can he handle this? I finally cross into his silence. "You're not thinking of getting down to the river from here."

Tyler shakes his head. He points to the right. "I've been down this way a few times before."

I follow him to an easier slope. Easier, but not easy. No marked trail here. "You think Paris will do okay?" I ask.

"He's going to have to. Besides, a wolf is more surefooted than a human any day." Tyler's boot slides and he falls back.

"Careful!" I call out.

"You be careful too," Tyler answers as I grab a rock to steady myself. "Follow exactly where I go."

"For sure." It's a long way down—maybe two CN Towers or four Eiffel Towers. Still, I find myself rushing, sliding, half-running when I can. Why did Tyler go down this way before? I cut around a huge boulder. Was he part of the search party that found his mom? How awful would that be? I stutter my feet down a muddy path. What if this search finds a bad ending too? I grip the brush to help slow myself down.

Paris cannot be held back, and when Tyler and I stop for a breath, he pushes past us. I gasp as his paws slip out from under him and with a yelp he begins to roll. "Paris, Paris!" Over and over.

Tyler chases after him, picking out his footing as fast as he can. He closes the gap in about a minute but it means Paris drops down at least one Eiffel

Tower more. Finally Tyler throws himself on top of the dog.

No yelp, no yell, no sound. Only a pile of tangled wolf and human.

"Are you okay?" I shout.

Slowly they detangle. Both of them are covered in mud. Paris's neck wound bleeds, and a scratch across Tyler's cheekbone looks like a red stream in a swollen purple riverbank. Paris barks at me. The bark sounds apologetic but hopeful. I pick my way down to join them.

"That was scary." I stop near Tyler and look more closely at his wound. "Do you have some first-aid equipment in your bag?"

"Sure. But let's just get to the bottom. We can wash out the scratches in the river."

"Slowly!" I yell at Paris as we start down again but I might as well tell the rapids to stop rushing. Down, down, down again; it takes forever when you have to be careful and watch your footing. We're almost at the bottom when my left ankle twists the wrong way against a rock. "Ow, geez, ouch." It's a one-second accident, just an awkward turn, not the endless tumble Paris took. Still, it leaves me breathing against the pain.

Tyler turns and looks into my eyes, his face tight with worry. "How bad is it?"

I shrug my shoulders. "It's nothing, really."
Another step forward and I wince.

"Can you make it down, or should I come back
up?"

I take a few more breaths. "I'm good." I lean
against a boulder as I limp slowly down the rest of
the way. When I make it to the bottom, I take another
deep breath.

"Clearly you are not 'good.' We aren't going to
be able to search for Martin with you like this,"
Tyler says.

"Maybe if I take the boot off and stick my foot
into the water, it'll numb the pain."

"Uh huh—there's a chance your ankle will swell
up and you won't be able to get the boot back on
again."

"I guess I better not. I'll be fine; I can do this,
don't worry. Let's fix you up." We find a rock to sit
on, and Paris laps at the water. The sun feels warm
down here, and most of the mist has burned off.
Just wisps are left, drifting off the ground and water.
Who could believe the weather could change so fast?
In between the wisps, the water sparkles with white
diamonds. I suddenly feel dopey and just want to
stretch back and rest. I have to fight to stay alert.

Tyler crouches at the bank and splashes water
over his cut. Then he removes a small red box from

his backpack and dabs white gauze against the top of a small brown bottle of antiseptic.

"Here, let me do it." I take the gauze from his hand and dab it along his wound. He jerks away and I see his eyes water. Before I can help myself, I lean over and kiss his cheekbone, this time with my lips.

His eyes widen and he grabs my wrists. Then he looks into my eyes, smiles, and kisses my lips so gently that I hardly believe our lips are touching. The sun, the air, his eyes—they all make me forget Zane and my brother for a moment.

But the moment passes. I break away and clear my throat. "We better get going."

"I'm going to try to clean Paris up first. Can you help me?" Tyler brings out a granola bar to lure Paris close, and I throw my arms around my pet wolf. Tyler takes off his jacket and strips off his T-shirt.

I try to look away. I don't feel I know him well enough to look at his bare chest, although guys are so much different about that kind of stuff. He's already tanned and he's lean, not one of those hairy, beary kind of mountain men. He's perfect, really.

Tyler dunks the shirt into the rushing water and then pushes it against Paris's bleeding gash. "That should stop the flow."

"You've ruined your shirt."

"Worth it." He wraps some bandage tape around the wound. "He can't chew at it from that angle."

Satisfied, Tyler smiles and looks up. His smile straightens immediately. "Oh my gosh. Look over there. Is that what I think it is?"

I turn in the direction that he's pointing. The mist has totally evaporated now and the sun glints off something red and big. I release Paris and limp toward it, closer and closer. Paris races ahead, barking and wagging his tail. I make out the four fat black wheels of the ATV, which is overturned. I stop.

"If Martin's underneath all that..."

"Never mind—keep going." Paris burrows underneath the vehicle. Tyler catches up and crawls underneath too. I would feel something inside if Martin was crushed under there, wouldn't I? We haven't lived together long, but we used to be so close. He still finishes my thoughts, sings the songs that are in my head; I should be able to sense whether he's alive or dead. But I don't feel anything except dread. I limp slower and slower toward them. A bad ending: this is what it could all come to right now, and I'm not ready. I have to count to be strong. One step, two, three steps, four.

"It's all right, he's not here."

Oh my God. My knees dissolve, I'm so relieved. I catch myself before I sink to the ground, and let go the breath I didn't know I was holding. Shading my eyes, I scan the riverbank. "But if he's not underneath the ATV, where did he go?"

"Never mind that for now. Let's try to turn this thing over. Ready on three. One...two...three."

I groan as we heave the ATV over onto its tires again. "Look, he left the keys in the ignition."

Tyler jumps in and turns them. The engine turns over a few times and then sputters out.

"If it worked, don't you think Martin would have driven it out?"

"If he figured out a way to flip it back over." Tyler's mouth buckles. He's thinking that if Martin were okay, he might have driven it off, but if he were hurt, unconscious, or something worse, he wouldn't have been able to. "Remember it was raining and the dampness wouldn't be a help, especially with carburetor problems." Tyler tries again. Nothing. And again. "C'mon, c'mon..." The engine sputters to life. "Yes! Climb in," Tyler yells at me. "Not you, Paris!"

"Paris, boy, listen to me." I hold his muzzle while I talk to him so his attention is on me. "You need to find Martin." But when I release him and the ATV rolls, he barks and seems more excited just to race it.

"Training," Tyler shouts over the engine. "Search-and-rescue dogs train for hours every week. We can't expect miracles."

But I can hope for one, I think, as we chug along slowly. I scan the right-hand side: rocks, brush, a spray of flowers like a quick promise. He's okay. I know he is. Or do I? Is that just wishing, or do I feel it? I can't be sure. Tyler scans the way ahead. Paris lopes alongside, by the river.

"So you figure Martin just walked away from the crash?" I ask, as I notice the crumpled front of the vehicle.

"No. I'm hoping he jumped out before the crash. You know, sensed he was losing control and going over so..." His words trail off and drown in the engine noise.

In my mind I can picture that—I see the ATV slide off the cliff trail, hear my brother shout with exhilaration as he leaps away from it. Sure, it would have been an adventure for him, like stumbling on a bear. He'd love it. "Idiot," I grumble. "Why didn't he stay with the ATV?"

"That would have been the smart thing to do. But remember how cold and rainy it was, even until a couple of hours ago. Maybe he thought he was close, went off, got disoriented..." Paris suddenly barks joyfully and tears ahead. He splashes into the icy, racing water.

"Come back here, you stupid dog. No time for swimming now."

Paris shakes something in his muzzle as he scrambles out.

"Tell me that isn't a fish." Smell aside, I know Paris catching and eating a fish won't affect me the way him chewing on a baby rabbit did. I can chuckle over this one, marvel even at how a dog can be so quick as to grab one of those slippery silver trout in his mouth.

"Is that Martin's shoe?" Tyler asks me as he stops the ATV, engine still running.

"Can't be, can it?" Still, as I jump down and wrestle Paris for the article, I know for certain it's not a fish. It's a gray, waterlogged, skater-type shoe, the heel all squished down in the back where Martin has squeezed his foot in a hundred times or more without undoing the laces. "Why would it be in the water?" A feeling slides down through me, like my heart, liver, stomach, and bowels are all going to leave me. That's why I felt that choking sensation yesterday, the needles in my mouth. Martin was in the water.

"I don't know why." Tyler's voice trembles, and he makes a great effort to recover for my sake. "Maybe he twisted his foot like you and wanted to soak it...and dropped the sneaker."

"Yeah, that could be it, you know. When we were little, we always hurt ourselves together. I'd bang up

my left knee, he'd scrape his right one. Martin probably twisted his ankle, just like me." I smile hopefully.

He nods. "Who really knows? Still, I think we
should head back to the cabin and call in the aquatic
rescue team."

Another picture snaps into my brain. The ATV
crashing over the edge of the trail and Martin
spilling out, bouncing on the rocks, and rolling into
the water. I don't even know if it's a true feeling or
image I'm having. I wish for the hundredth time that
our parents hadn't separated us when we were ten.
I don't even want to imagine anymore. I put my head
down in my hands. Paris jumps up on the ATV, wagging and licking at my legs. "You have to find him,
boy. That's the only way you can make me feel better."

Tyler leans over and takes me into his arms. I
know he has to be thinking the same thing. I can
feel myself caving into him and hear myself sobbing.
But I feel like part of me has totally left my body.

CHAPTER 15

_____

"C'MON, WE JUST DON'T KNOW WHAT HAPPENED. IT'S TOO soon to cry. Let's try to pull together and think this through. Do you think you can make it back up the hill the way we came?"

I can feel a hot ache inside my boot and pull up my right pant leg to look. Even at the top of the boot, the skin puffs out like a sausage escaping its casing.

I shake my head. "Sorry."

"That's okay, we can come back for the truck. As long as this thing has enough gas, we can make it out of here. We'll continue along the river until the climb's not so steep. Then we'll try to get this baby up the escarpment. With luck, we'll join the Ribbon Glacier Trail and be home in no time."

But luck isn't really with me today, we all know that. Otherwise I'd be standing in a gallery in Paris right now, sipping something sparkly, looking at Mom's paintings. After ten minutes, we can hear the engine cough and hesitate. We keep going, Paris weaving ahead from the river to the scrub and brush on the mountain side of the ATV. Tyler slows the machine down to conserve gas, and Paris disappears completely.

The ATV gives a large hiccup and then rolls to a stop.

"Oh fine, now what?"

Tyler's face turns red, like this is all his fault. He tries to turn the engine over again, but it doesn't even give a little gasp. "Okay, we're not going to make the same mistake as your brother. We won't leave the ATV." He opens up his backpack and grabs a flare. "First, we'll light one of these. Here, hold it." I take it from him and he fumbles through his bag for a sealed box of matches. The first one he strikes quickly blows out. For the next, we both reach out to cup our spare hands around the fuse and the flame as he makes the two connect.

A sizzly, firecracker sound starts up as the flame ignites. "Wish I had a flare gun. Oh well, here goes." He flings the flare up high into the sky at an angle. His pitching arm works well. Like an oversize birthday sparkler, the flare crackles bits of lightning against the pale blue sky as it soars up, up toward the sun hanging over the river. Then it arcs slowly and streaks down to the river, smoke trailing after it.

"I didn't want to start a fire so I aimed it in that direction," Tyler explains.

"Is there anything else we can do?" I ask.

"Well, now we can take off your boot and soak that foot, for one thing. Wish I knew where Paris went. Probably scaring up trouble somewhere."

I bend over to unlace my boot, gasping with the additional pressure forced into the ankle area.

"Here, you can put your leg up on my knee."

I brace myself for the pain and then lift. "Ow, crap. Why did I have to slip on that rock?"

Tyler shrugs and flashes me his blue-eyed sympathy. His lips straighten, a smile without humor.

He quickly undoes the laces and loosens them, pulling the sides of the boots open to give my swelling ankle room. "Okay, now put your arms around my neck and I'll carry you to the river." He leans closer and slips one arm under my legs, the other around my back.

While I'm thin, bony even, I'm still long, and it's heavy and awkward for Tyler to hoist me up as he straightens and climbs out of the ATV. He takes the five steps to the river, then puts me down on a rock.

He unlaces his own boots and pulls them and his socks off. Then he removes mine. I put an arm around his neck and hop into the river.

"Easy," Tyler warns, "we don't want to fall; the current's pretty fast."

"Yeah, I remember." I dip my foot, and the glacier-cold water brings instant relief. In a second, I don't feel as though I have any feet, or ankles, for that matter.

We stand that way for five minutes, not speaking. His arm around my back feels as though it belongs there, my arm around his neck feels comfortable. He holds me closer and kisses me. I feel like I'm flowing into the cold water; his lips are the only warmth I sense.

I throw my other arm around him. There's nothing else but this sensation of his lips touching mine. I hear something—a snuffle? I break away. "Paris?"

"Oh my God." Tyler pulls away. "Don't move, don't say anything. Just hold on in case we have to run."

I wince. About a truck-length away, two huge bears amble into the water, one a honey color, the other chocolate. The honey-colored bear laps at the water; the chocolate-colored one rakes his paw through it, splashing the other.

The lighter-colored bear stops drinking and straightens. His lip curls back to show huge yellow fangs. His growl rattles right through my bones. With one massive paw, he cuffs the chocolate-colored bear.

"I'm going to carry you to the ATV now," Tyler whispers. "Whatever you do, don't make a sound."

The dark-brown bear rears back and throws himself at the other one.

One step at a time, Tyler takes us out of the icy water. He's holding me so he can't really see his feet, but we both hear when one connects with a branch. Even over the sound of the water, it sounds like a firecracker going off.

The bears stop wrestling and turn in our direction. The dark-brown one opens his mouth and teeth into an ugly snarl. The light-brown one lopes toward us.

I look around. How high would I have to climb to be out of the reach of those massive paws speeding toward us? It's hopeless—the closest trees are short, scruffy firs. Besides, my swollen foot wouldn't grip any kind of trunk enough to climb it. "You go ahead and make a break for it."

"Shut up!" Tyler snaps, as he breaks the speed of light to get us to the ATV. He drops me there and rifles through his backpack. The honey-colored bear is still running in our direction. I duck down behind the ATV as if that will help.

Tyler pulls out a flashlight and flings it at the honey-colored bear. The hard plastic casing bounces off a rock and splits in two. The clear window pings off and hits the bear, and the battery and bottom splash into the water, wetting and startling the snarling creature a second time. His snarl changes to a yowl, more of a whine than a threat. The chocolate-colored bear stands up on his hind feet and roars. The honey-colored bear changes his course and swerves away, heading back to the brush.

The dark-brown one gives another roar and then lopes off after him.

"Oh man, I thought we were in for a fight there," Tyler says.

"But bears aren't supposed to bother people, remember?"

"Yeah, well, define 'bother.' I didn't want to argue a finer point about bear etiquette with either of those two."

"Wonder if Martin has seen a bear yet?" I say quietly. I block pictures trying to form in my brain—my goofy, wild brother chasing into the trees, going out of his way to find a two-ton terror with fur.

"I'm sure he's going to have a few stories for us when we all get out of this."

If he gets out of this, I can't help thinking.

Tyler puts his socks and boots back on and hands me mine. I sit down and slip into the right one easily. The left one just sits there.

"Hungry?" Tyler is already rummaging through his backpack and brings out a couple of apples. He tosses me one and I catch it.

Nothing tastes better. The apple snaps between my teeth, splashing juice around my face. I can't hear anything over the sound of my own crunching.

Tyler jabs my shoulder. "Listen!"

A strange, rhythmic, mechanical noise. Helicopter blades?

Tyler drops his apple core and fumbles for another flare. The helicopter circles away. Agonizingly slowly, Tyler strikes a match and holds it to the wick. It blows out. The helicopter looks like a large insect flying off toward the horizon. He lights another and we cup it together again. Out again. Another match. We use our bodies to shelter it this time. The flame touches the wick. Nothing, nothing. Finally a small glow ignites the wick. The sizzling begins. "Cross your fingers." After a quick inhale, he pitches the flare into the air. Not as high or as far as last time; still, it leaves a long, lasting trail of smoke. Someone in that helicopter just has to look back for a second.

The helicopter keeps blending the sky with its propeller till it becomes a tiny speck...and then nothing.

"So close. Damn!" Everything inside me slides down. I feel a tear on my cheek.

"We're fine. Don't worry." Tyler shuffles over and throws an arm around me. "We've got food, it's warm.

Worst comes to worst, we can soak your ankle some more and head back up the mountain to the truck."

Tyler grins. "Nuts to the caffeine. A T-bone steak sizzling on a barbecue."

"Tabbouleh salad with a tofu kebab," I sigh.

"Hot-fudge sundae."

It strikes me that we both had a big breakfast. Why are we so hungry? The sun is slipping down in the sky—it must be way past lunch. "What time is it anyway?" I ask Tyler.

He looks at his watch. "Two o'clock."

"They'll be wondering where we're at by now."

"Unless they're all out searching for Martin." Tyler squeezes my shoulder. "Doesn't matter—they'll find us at the same time."

"But where's Paris?" I start to holler. "Paris! Paris!" No crashing in the bushes, only the soft shushing of the water over the rocks answering me. I stick two fingers in the corners of my mouth and whistle as loud and as long as I can, just as I did at the Rocky Mountain Wolf Haven. Nothing.

"He may be gone permanently. His little vacation at the retreat may have helped him discover his inner wolf."

I frown. How can being torn into by fellow members of his species help him turn wild? With us, he was taken care of, fed, bandaged, and loved. I whistle again, louder and longer. And again. Then, as if I summoned it, a helicopter warbles in the distance and appears to drift closer.

"They're coming back for us! They must have seen us!" Tyler leaps up and performs a jumping jack to make sure. Closer and closer, the helicopter hovers.

I look around. "Where do you think it will land?"

"Land? Here, with the rocks and the brush? Are you crazy? They're going to throw us a line."

"Throw us a line," I repeat weakly, even as I see a cable lower. I swallow hard as the helicopter swings around and hovers directly above us.

"Listen, you go on up." Tyler grabs hold of the metal rope, which is just above his head by now. He catches the harness dangling from the end. "Tell them I'll head back up the cliff and drive the truck to the Park Office. Make sure they know about the ATV and the shoe Paris found in the water." He reaches his hand out for me, to help me up.

"Tyler, I can't."

CHAPTER 16

"THERE'S NO TIME TO ARGUE. THE HELICOPTER ONLY CARRIES so much fuel. Here, I'll help you with the straps."

I shake my head. "You don't understand. I'll throw up. I'll pee myself. There's no way I can let myself be hoisted up to the helicopter. I can't deal with heights."

"You don't have a choice, Zanna."

I'm still shaking my head.

Tyler grabs my chin. "You're wasting their time and your brother's chances."

Martin's still out there. I have to do this. I squeeze my eyes closed and then open them again. My teeth chatter as I lean against Tyler to step into the harness.

"Better put this on too." Tyler opens the boot for my right foot and I stuff it in. He makes a loose knot and then double-checks my harness straps. "You ready?" He looks into my eyes, waiting.

I swallow and nod. The wind plasters my hair back. The roar of the helicopter engine drowns out all other sound. Tyler waves an okay signal at the chopper. Tug, tug! Whoo! I grip the cable and my knees dissolve. My heart feels like it's in my ears.

Instantly my body is lifted from the ground. Up, up, up. As the helicopter rises, Tyler grows smaller, his encouraging smile and wink tinier and farther away. It's like I'm fading from the earth's memory. The ground swirls. I'm not all that good on a Ferris wheel, or any other ride high in the air, for that matter. Slowly I'm reeled up, the human fish on the helicopter's line. I swing in the air. Up, up.

As my body passes the feet of the chopper, someone grabs me under my armpits and helps me in. I fold over with relief and just breathe for a while.

My father removes some earphones. "Are you all right?" he shouts.

"I twisted my ankle," I yell back.

Down below, Tyler waves off the helicopter with a tiny arm.

"It's okay, he wants to go back up the cliff and get his truck," I explain to the guy who helped me into the cabin. The pilot nods, and the chopper slowly pulls away.

"I've lost my dog—have you seen him?" I ask as I peer through the glass. My stomach feels swirly.

The guy shakes his head. "Should we head over to the hospital for some x-rays?" He directs the question at Dad, like I shouldn't be allowed to decide for myself, so I answer to Dad because he's obviously the one who will give the final word.

"No, honestly, don't waste the time. Dad, I'm fine. I'll just put my foot up. Listen, we found the other ATV overturned on the rocks, and Paris found Martin's shoe in the water."

My father's mouth drops open, and his cheeks sag. He runs a hand over his face.

The pilot immediately hails someone on his radio and repeats what I just told them. When he's done, he turns to us. "They're bringing the search party to the river and adding an aquatic rescue unit."

"What do you want to do, Doc?" the winch man asks.

"Take us to the hospital."

"Dad, no. We'll lose time. We have to find Martin."

"Zanna, there are good people looking for him. We need to have your ankle checked. And we need to call your mother. She needs to know what's happening."

My mother, who is probably sipping a lovely French wine as she accepts compliments from art groupies, needs to know what? That we're searching for Martin but it doesn't look good? A sneaker in the water—what does that usually mean?

But Martin's a great swimmer.

Still, I remember the numbing effect of the icy water on my ankle earlier, and the way the water sucked at me yesterday when I fell in. The needle sensation when I tried to breathe. The way the river current controlled me and made me feel that struggling was hopeless, that I could never get out. The bumps and knocks of the stones in the water. Any of these things could have knocked me out. I had Tyler to save me. Martin had no one.

And where's Paris? I wonder for the hundredth time as I lean toward the helicopter window. I swallow down my motion sickness. A scrubby tree here, a bush there. Rocks, a mountain, great wilderness scenery, all in miniature, the way I like it. If it were all stuffed in a glass globe, I could shake it and it would snow. Today I want to shake it to produce my brother and my dog. But no luck. Both have been swallowed up: Martin by the river, Paris by the wild.

Dad doesn't use his satellite phone in the air but waits till we land at the hospital. While we're in the emergency room waiting area, he uses a pay phone. It takes forever: four separate phone calls. A call to Mom's flat, a call to the gallery, a call to Jacques' cell phone, and then a call back to a private office number at the gallery. I can tell by his face as he talks what he thinks has happened to Martin.

He winces and tries to control his voice, which breaks despite his efforts. "Joanna, we can't find him. He may have fallen into the water."

I crumple in my chair nearby, crying quietly to myself.

After he slips the receiver back into the cradle, he comes over, kneels, and hugs me hard. I can feel his shoulders shake and realize I have to be strong for him. "Dad, it will be okay. Martin didn't drown. No way. You know we have that twin thing going for us? Well, I know. He's out there somewhere."

Dad pulls away. "I hope so, Zanna. Your mother's taking the first flight out tomorrow."

"Why not today?" A sudden fierce realization flares inside me from the pit of my stomach up into my throat. I want—*need* my mother here. Right now!

"I don't know, honey. Maybe there are no seats available. She's looking into it."

She's enjoying the rest of her opening night, that's why she can't fly today. I know my mother too well. Still, I can't help feeling a tiny lightness inside. The mother who used to be able to kiss anything better—maybe she can fix all this too. "So Mom should be here late tomorrow?"

"She'll call me with exact times as soon as she knows, so I can pick her up in Calgary."

Dad calls Drew next so that he can drive the truck over and pick us up.

The emergency doctor calls me in.

Dad claps a hand on my thigh. "Come on now. Let's see about that ankle."

I hate that a stupid little twist against a rock is making both of us lose time on the search for Martin. One second is all it takes: something goes wrong and it costs so much and there's no going back to fix it. I lean on Dad and hobble to the doctor's office.

The doctor wants an x-ray and as we wait for the results, Dad calls Cassandra to hear how the search is going. Apparently, boats can't navigate the rapids of Ribbon River so the search party is divided up along the two banks, pacing along the sides, scanning for articles of clothing. Nothing so far, which I hope is a good thing. The thought comes to me suddenly: *they're all searching in the wrong place.*

The x-ray confirms that my ankle isn't broken. "Just keep it up, and alternate ice and heat on it," the doctor says as she tapes it. She also hands me some crutches. "Try those for size."

I slip the wide parts under my armpits. "Perfect. Let's go, Dad. Let's get back on the search."

"No weight on that at all, says the doctor. If you can help it, stay off your feet."

"I can't help it!" I snap. "We're searching for my brother." I navigate my way out to the front with Dad at my side.

Drew's waiting for us in the truck. Still no news about Martin. "Where to, Doc?"

"Home. We'll drop Zanna off."

Drew takes us out of the hospital parking lot.

"Dad, I can't just sit at the cabin. Paris is missing too. Maybe if we find him, he can help us find Martin."

"Let me think. I have to think." I can see Dad's exhausted. His eyes are glazed and red, like he's sick. "We have to go home anyway—the ATVs are there. You really have to stay back, Zanna."

I don't argue. Neither of us can take it. Still, as I recognize the main drag of Last Chance and see we're going to pass the Park Office, I tell Dad to stop the truck. "I want to see if Tyler made it back okay."

Drew rolls the truck up to the door, and it takes me a few minutes to get out. I know what I'm going to do. I need to convince Tyler to head back out with me. We can wait till Dad is gone and take another quad. Slowly, I crutch and hop my way into the office. Tyler's on the phone. My feet and crutches keep swinging toward the computers at the back. For something to do, I check my e-mail. *What could Zane possibly have to say that could make me feel better?* I wonder, but it's not so much that. Checking e-mail is routine, habit, comfort, addiction even, as my mother would be quick to tell me.

I sign on and download, all the time watching to
see if Tyler's off the phone. No mail, not even a note
from The Artiste, my mother.

I start one.

Zane. Everything's gone so wrong. Martin's
missing somewhere near Ribbon Glacier.
Everybody thinks he's drowned. I can't, won't,
don't believe it! I'll keep searching the rest of
my life if I have to. Wish you were here.

But do I really wish Zane was here, I wonder? I
stop and look over at Tyler whose telephone conversation ends in that moment. He gets up and glances my
way. I can't even try to smile. Not now, when I don't
know what's happened to Martin. But if anyone could
make me feel better, I know it would be Tyler, not
Zane.

I'll call you in a couple of days, one way or the
other, to let you know how things turn out.
Love, Zanna

I sign off and hump-swing my way toward Tyler.

"Not broken, I see?" Tyler points to my taped-up
ankle.

"Just a sprain. And you made it back up that

mountain. Amazing," I tell him.

"Never any doubt." He pauses and frowns. "Any exciting e-mail?" Tyler's voice sounds flat—bet he's exhausted too.

"No. All the excitement's definitely happening here, unfortunately. You didn't spot Paris anywhere on your way back?"

Tyler shakes his head. "I hoped you'd find him curled up on the balcony of the cabin when you went back."

I pause: that makes sense, like in all those animal stories where dogs or cats cross mountains and streams for thousands of miles just to return to their owners. "We haven't been home yet. Listen, Tyler, I have to find him." I push through the gate at the counter so that I can stand by him at the desk.

Tyler stands up. "Oh, you think you can find Martin better than the search parties?"

I frown at him, confused. What's happened to him? He's back to sounding like he disapproves of the city girl again. "Maybe. I'm not sure if I just want him not to be in the river where everyone's looking, or whether I'm getting a vibe from him that he's somewhere different. Still, I'm the only one who can get Paris in. And Paris can find Martin better than any stranger, right?"

"I suppose." Dense and rock-stubborn, his jaw juts out.

"Well, then, can you help me?"

"I don't think so, Zanna." He stares down at the floor.

I sigh. "You're tired, I know. Dad shouldn't go out either, he's wiped. Maybe I can grab Drew or Jason. I don't want to go out alone."

Tyler looks up. "You shouldn't go out at all."

"Why not? I can put my foot up in the ATV. I'll even put a pack of frozen peas on my ankle."

"Not because of your injury. Because Martin is your brother...because you might find him..." I see the flash of pain cross his face before he can force all his features flat again. His eyes wince, his mouth buckles, then they straighten. He stares at the floor again.

"You found your mother." I say it gently, not even as a question.

He nods.

I reach my arms around him and hold him. "I'm sorry, Tyler." I kiss his cheek. "But you survived, and you know how you felt then. You had to search."

"You're never the same," he whispers. "You don't know what it's like. Everything is dead afterward."

"If I'm not there when they find him, do you think anything will be the same for me? He's my brother, my twin brother, for God's sake."

He shakes his head. "The other way is worse,

trust me. You'll never get it out of your head."

"I have to go!" I repeat. "Paris may come if I call him. He won't return for anyone on the search party."

Tyler won't answer.

"If you don't help me, you know I'll go out anyway."

"Fine," he answers. "Let me call my dad. He's on the riverbank with the others."

I wait as he uses the desk phone to call his father. He turns away from me and talks in a low tone he hopes I won't hear. "Nothing yet. Well, that's good, I guess. I'm going to go over the Ribbon Glacier Trail with an ATV. No, I'll make sure it's got gas. Okay. See you."

I don't even explain to Dad why Tyler's following us in the Park truck, and Dad doesn't ask. My ankle throbs in my boot as the truck bumps over the dirt road. I imagine it flashing like a lightbulb. On, the pain shoots red-hot for a moment; off, the pain subsides.

I also imagine that Tyler is right. Curled up at the glass patio door, Paris will lie waiting for us to come pat and feed him. I can see it in my mind. He'll leap up and go crazy when he sees us. Then we'll sneak out again in the ATV, and somewhere along the way, Paris will pick up Martin's scent. He'll run, we'll follow, and at the end of the scent...some kind of shelter? I can't imagine anything further.

If only Dad would drive faster.... Everything takes so much longer when you're anxious. Still, if Paris is waiting for us around the next bend, on that balcony overlooking the lake, I'll take it as a sign that maybe my luck has changed and my brother is alive.

When we finally pull into the driveway at the back of the cabins, I jump out immediately and hump-swing myself down to the cabin calling, "Paris! Paris!"

Tyler pulls in beside our truck and runs to join me. But it's already clear as I look around calling: my luck hasn't changed.

There are no wolves here.

CHAPTER 17

TYLER'S THE ONE WHO HEATS UP A COUPLE OF CANS OF chicken soup for Dad and me; we're both so depressed. I don't say anything about the chicken. I'll just leave it in the bowl, I decide. I tell him where to find the bread and pea butter, and we all sit on the stools, my left leg taking up a seat of its own.

Dad spreads some of the pea butter on his bread and takes a bite. "Geez, this stuff is awful," he mumbles as he tries to pull the bottom part of his mouth away from the top.

"What did you expect? You hate peanut butter," I tell him.

"I thought it would taste a little more...exotic. Let me grab some sardines from the cupboard." Dad slides off his chair and reaches to open the cabinet door. He slaps a small, flat can and a triangular metal wedge-shaped one—Spam—on the counter. Then he grabs three cans of pop from the fridge.

As he sips his pop, head in his hand, Dad seems to slump lower and lower. His eye lids close. Still sitting up, he begins to snore. I can't believe my luck.

"Quick, let's go!" I whisper to Tyler.

Tyler grabs the food from the counter and stuffs it in the backpack. Then he opens the freezer, pulls out a bag of frozen peas, and tosses them to me. "For your ankle. Go show me how you put your foot up in that vehicle."

"Out the window, on the door, you'll see. The yellow ATV's a four-seater with storage space." Still, I know I'm in no shape to move quickly. When he's not looking, I poke a hole in the bag and pour some of the frozen peas into my boot. That feels great. It won't look or smell pretty later, I'm sure. But if it helps me get my brother back faster, who cares?

I grab the keys to the yellow ATV from the hook in Dad's bedroom and we head out. Tyler helps me climb into the vehicle. I unsnap a window and hang my leg out.

"Trouble is, we can't hear Paris over the engine sounds," Tyler says as the engine rumbles to life.

"We'll have to stop every once in a while and listen."

"But Paris can hear me, right? I mean, wolves have great hearing, don't they?"

"I don't know. You can try calling."

The engine grumbles and roars so loudly I can't hear myself, so I give that up right away. "Can I borrow your whistle?" I ask Tyler, and he pushes the backpack towards me.

"Side pocket." He points.

I take it out and blow as loudly as I can. Over and over. The shriek of the whistle sounds confident and commanding, and it feels good to be trying something, anything. We bump onto the trail from the road, and drive to where the edge crests over the river.

"This is where Cassandra thought she saw something red," I shout at Tyler. "Where we stopped last night." I grab Tyler's arm so he understands to park the ATV.

He steers it to the river side of the trail and hops out. Then he circles around to help me. I pull my left leg out of the window and pour more frozen peas down the boot.

"Down that way is where we found the red ATV. But really, you know how fast and hard Paris can run. He could be on the other side of the park, for all we know."

I begin calling as I crutch and hobble my way around: "Paris, Paris!" And then just in case, "Martin!"

Tyler studies the brush on the river side of the path. "Hey, Zanna. I found where Martin may have left the path."

I limp to where he crouches. Large tire marks arc off the trail, through some trampled brush, over the slope. It's not that high, I tell myself, even as I feel pea butter sandwich backing up in my throat. Martin could have survived. "Do you think Martin was thrown into the river?"

"Worst-case scenario," Tyler answers.

"But you know, I think I would feel different if he was down there. I'm almost positive he's someplace else. Let's go for the best case. Paris! Paris! Damn that dog."

I hobble and crutch along the other side of the trail away from the river, my favorite scenario. I blow into Tyler's whistle, again and again. Tyler slips and slides along the river side. Out of frustration, I whistle long and hard using my thumb and forefinger, and stumble over a rock. "Ow, ouch, crap!" I sprawl across the ground.

Tyler rushes over. "Are you okay?"

"I'm fine, really. It's just hard to navigate with these crutches." My arm bleeds from the branch that ripped across it as I fell.

"You're not fine! This is ridiculous."

"Shhh!" I struggle to get up again.

"Don't shush me. I'm taking you home right now."

I punch his knee. It's as high as I can reach. "I hear something. Listen!" It's not another bear, it can't be. I whistle long and hard again, and then grab onto Tyler's leg and hoist myself up. A wolf howls back.

"Do you think that's who I think it is?"

"A normal wolf wouldn't answer a human whistle. It has to be. C'mon." Tyler grabs my arm and we try a three-legged race toward the sound. "Arooooo!" When it stops, I whistle again.

The howl seems to come from the mountainside itself. I keep hump-swinging toward it. The next howl comes from a rock. It's eerie. Tyler runs ahead and disappears into the mountain. I squint and keep thumping along.

Paris appears and runs toward me, wagging his tail.

"Paris!" I kneel down and he pushes me over. I let him lick me till I hear Tyler call.

"Zanna! Over here!"

"Over where?" His voice seems to come straight from the mountain.

"Behind the rock."

I draw closer.

"Martin's here." Tyler's voice sounds steady but flat. Why isn't he happier?

I can't breathe. I don't ask the question but I need to know. I pull myself up on Paris. Together we head toward his voice.

As I step around a huge boulder, I see that Tyler's crouching down at the mouth of a small cave. He's got his canteen out. Surely Martin has to be alive if he's offering him a drink.

"Martin!" He lies still in front of Tyler in the cave. I hold my breath as I step to Tyler's side. The right side of Martin's face is unrecognizable—swollen, purple, his eye a slash in the swelling.

"Go back. Really, Zanna, you don't want to see."

My eyes fix on Martin's mouth: is it opening, closing? And then his chest. Is it moving? I don't see anything. My chest aches and I can't breathe. Despite what Tyler says, my eyes take in the rest of Martin's body. His right arm is scraped raw and bloody. His jeans are torn and appear to be oozing dark, purple-red blood. Worse still, something pokes out just below his knee. A piece of white bone.

CHAPTER 18

"ZANNA, ZANNA, DON'T PASS OUT ON ME!" TYLER BEGS.

I force my eyes open.

"He looks really bad but I found a pulse."

I crouch down quickly. "What should we do?"

"I don't know." He lowers his voice. "Martin must have crawled up from the river himself. That should mean he doesn't have a spinal-cord injury. We could take the chance and move him. He needs help badly." Tyler winces. "Or should I go back and get a chopper to airlift him out?"

"The chopper would hoist him up. Oh my God, Tyler."

"He won't care. He'll be on a stretcher, and he's out right now. If he wakes up enough...it might be a shock."

"How long do you think it'd be before they'd come?"

Tyler shakes his head. "Too long. You know what, I'm going to splint that leg, and we'll take him out. Stay here a minute while I bring the ATV closer."

Alone with my brother for a moment, I force

myself to look at his uninjured side. That side looks almost normal, as if he were just sleeping.

"Martin, Martin!" I call gently.

Behind the uninjured eyelid, it looks as if his eye is moving.

"Zanna." A hoarse whisper, but his lips haven't moved, have they?

I don't trust my ears.

"Martin?" I whisper.

His right eye flashes open but his iris floats around and doesn't focus on me. His lips move but I can't hear anything. I lean forward.

"I saw..." His lip stretches—he can't be smiling, can he? "Two bears."

"Oh, you!" I'd swat him but he looks in such rough shape. Instead, I feel tears slide down my face.

The rumble of the ATV announces Tyler's arrival. He scrambles out with a large, thick branch in his hand and a rope in the other.

"Martin's awake," I tell him.

"Mmm—might be better for this if he wasn't. Can you distract him?

I see him put the branch next to Martin's leg.

"So Martin, what happened?" I talk brightly to my brother, who seems out again anyway. "I mean, were you stunt-riding or what?"

He opens his lips to answer but groans instead, then cries out sharply and slumps. Tyler winces.

"Done. Okay, quick, while he's out. On three, you grab his shoulders, and we'll hoist him to the ATV. One...two...three." Tyler scoops Martin up, one arm under his hips, the other under his legs for support.

I climb backward into the backseat of the ATV, ignoring the hot flash of pain in my own ankle. I sit holding the top half of Martin on my lap. Tyler scrambles around and into the driver's seat and we rumble off, Paris loping alongside. It doesn't take long: ironically, in terms of distance, Martin has never been that far away.

"Dad, Dad!" I call as the ATV pulls up to the cabin.

"Oh my God, Zanna. Where the hell were you?" Dad runs onto the deck at the front of the cabin and pounds down the stairs two at a time.

"We found Martin!"

"What?" I've never seen him move as fast as he does loping toward us. "Thank God," he says as he draws close, and then his breath catches when he sees the shape Martin's in.

"Martin, Martin." His words come out in a rush. He brushes his hand gently over the top of my brother's hair. "We're going to have to get you to a hospital." He talks to Tyler and me now. "Let's move him to the truck, in the back where he can lie flat."

"I'll get his comforter and pillow," I suggest.

"Let me," Tyler answers. "I better take Paris into the cabin too."

I stay seated in the ATV, my brother heavy in my arms; still, I'm so glad to feel his weight and presence. It makes me feel like I'm doing something, anything, just helping in some small way. When Tyler gets back, he and Dad hoist Martin carefully into the truck. As I straighten and get out, my body sparks with pins and needles, as though all my nerve endings are awakening from a deep sleep.

With my ankle flashing on and off with a dull ache, I position the pillow and tuck the comforter around Martin. Then I throw in my crutches and Tyler helps me into the back so that I can ride with my brother.

"Right. Good luck." Tyler looks uncomfortable about leaving, like he wants to do or say something more. "I'm going to head back in the Park truck and let everyone know what's happening."

"Right, we're off." Dad climbs into the truck and pulls onto the road. I wave to Tyler as he drives off too.

Heading to the Last Chance Hospital in the back with Martin, it's a long, slow, bumpy ride and the sun is setting. It's getting cooler. As I watch Martin's reaction to every jolt, I sing softly because the silly words make me feel less scared for him. *My baby left me for a bodybuilder. She didn't want to live with a pipe welder. I've got the tools, he hangs around pools. I need to get a six-pack if I want my baby back. Oooooh!*

It makes him feel better too; I know, because he's my twin. A couple of tears slide down my cheek as I wonder how I ever lived without him back at my mom's apartment in Toronto. How can my mother live without the two of us?

When we get to the tiny hospital, attendants rush Martin into Emergency on a stretcher while we sit on red vinyl chairs waiting and hoping for good news.

Dad grabs a coffee and I sit flipping through magazines, the same issues I've flipped through in the dentist's waiting room back home in Toronto. *Back home, Toronto*: a million miles away, a million years away.

Finally a doctor comes out to talk to us. "We've sedated Martin and he's resting comfortably, but we're going to have to airlift him to Calgary. He has a concussion and his leg is badly broken. He's going to need surgery and we can't do that here."

"Do whatever you have to," Dad answers. "Thank you."

"I've already made the call for the helicopter. But it will take a while. In the meantime, you could take care of the paperwork and maybe even go home for some rest." The doctor leaves Dad with some forms.

His leg is badly broken. I remember that white piece of bone poking through his jeans and feel queasy. "They're not going to have to amputate, are they?" I ask Dad.

"Let's take this one step at a time, Zanna. He's alive, and that's better than what I imagined last night when I called your mother."

"What about Mom? When will she get here?"

"Shoot, I better call her. She'll want to know that we found Martin. Come on, let's find a phone."

It only takes one call this time to reach Mom, but it's about 2:00 A.M., Paris time. I can't hear the relief in her voice—I mean, Dad's the one on the phone with her. I can't figure out whether Dad has woken her, or whether she's been tossing and turning all night, hoping to hear from us.

When he hangs up, I say, "So, when will she be here?"

Dad smacks his forehead. "You know what? She didn't say anything and I forgot to ask. Let's call her tomorrow. We'll be in Calgary anyway, so we can swing round to the airport and pick her up whenever she arrives."

What he says makes sense, but I'm disappointed. What I most want to do is to call her back right now right away. I want to tell her everything we've been through, to shake her up as much as we've been shaken up, to make her understand how close we've come to losing Martin. Just in case she doesn't know.

"First chance I get, no matter what it takes, I'm going to make sure we get a telephone line in the cabin," Dad tells me next day as he tries for the fifth time to reach the hospital. "The damn satellite connection is so bad I can't hear a thing when I get the operator."

"Why don't we just stop in at the Park Office on our way to Calgary? We could ask Tyler to look after Paris while we're at the hospital. Or will Cassandra and the guys do it?"

"No, let's ask Tyler. The crew needs to cover for me and keep up with the readings. Yes, let's stop at the Park Office. That's a great idea."

"I'll let Paris out for a run first. Paris, here boy!" I head out to the front with him and onto the deck. In the distance, the lake shimmers with a million carats of sunshine.

Paris looks up at me, almost as though he needs permission to run off. I stoop down to talk to him.

"Paris, you saved Martin. There's no doubt in my mind. Without you, we would never have found him."

Paris licks his lips and yips like he's trying to answer back but can't.

"I'm sorry I put you in that wolf retreat." I put my arms around him, gently so as not to hurt his neck wound, and he licks my face. "It won't ever happen again. Trouble or not, you're part of our family." I hug and pat him again. "Now go for your run."

When Dad and I head for the truck, Paris hops in before we even realize he's there. At the Park Office, Tyler's dad doesn't say anything when we walk in with the dog, but I do.

"Mr. Benson," I say, holding on to Paris's scruff. "I know you don't allow animals in here. But Paris saved my brother's life. Do you think Tyler could look after him while we're in Calgary?"

Mr. Benson smiles and crouches down to pat Paris. "As far as I'm concerned, Paris isn't just some animal anymore. Are you, boy?" Paris wags his tail and licks Mr. Benson's fingers, and Mr. Benson looks up at me with an even bigger grin. "Paris is a rescue dog. Or wolf. And he's welcome here any time."

"Thank you. Is Tyler around? I'd like to talk to him."

"He's across the street at his grandmother's. He'll be back in five minutes."

The shabby house, the lady with the walker— she's his grandmother? There's so much I don't know about him. Even though it seems like I've known him a lifetime, it's only been a few days.

"Can we use your phone?" Dad asks. Mr. Benson motions him to the spare phone on the second desk.

"It's two o'clock in the afternoon. I guess your mother will be up now," Dad says, but he still has trouble reaching her. He tries the gallery and she picks up there. "Uh-huh, uh-huh. You're not coming?"

Not coming where? To Last Chance or Calgary? I wonder. I hear it in his voice. Dad finds Mom hard to believe. Not as much as I do, though. "Let me talk to her!" I screech at him.

He hands me the receiver.

"Hello, Mom." I bite down on the anger and the tears I have stored up.

"Hi, Zanna. How are you?"

"Mom, Mom, it's been awful." I choke on the words; it's so hard not to cry. "You should see Martin, he looks really bad. I thought he was dead." She's quiet at the other end. A long pause, and then all my disappointment and hurt solidifies into one question. "Why aren't you coming?"

"As I explained to your dad, there's no point in me visiting when your brother will be stuck in bed. I want to visit when I can take him places and do things."

"He needs you right now when he's sick."

"But the art show is still on."

"You're not coming because of an art show?"

"There are lots of buyers here. Zanna, this is how I make my living. I'm not like your dad—I don't have tenure at some university..."

"But you said you would come!"

"Yes, when your brother went missing, in the heat of the moment, I thought I had to be there. Really, you and your dad have things in hand now. What reason is there for me to be there?"

"Because you're my mom and I need you."

"I'm sorry, Zanna. I need things too."

She's a million miles away. I swallow hard. She's just not going to come, And there's nothing I can do to make her change her mind.

"I'll be there in September. We'll take a big shopping trip in Toronto and then you can fly out to France and live with me there. Would you like that, Zanna?"

A tear brands my cheek as it slides down into the corner of my mouth. I brush it away too late. Salted sadness flavors my mouth. "I can't talk anymore, Mom. The connection is fading." I don't even say good-bye; there's nothing good about it. I just slip the receiver back onto the cradle.

CHAPTER 19

STUPID HABIT. I CHECK FOR E-MAIL KNOWING THERE'S NOTH-ing from Zane. *You have no new mail*, the mailer tells me. I'm right. Still, I can't leave it that way. What if he read my note about Martin disappearing? I have to talk to him, if only to let him know my brother's okay. I get up and hump-swing my way to the front to borrow the phone. "Dad, I need to call Toronto."

Mr. Benson tells me to dial a special number so there won't be a long-distance charge.

I still remember Zane's number. I can't believe I didn't think to try him earlier. The phone rings again and again till his sister Imelda picks up.

"Hi, it's Zanna. Is Zane there?"

"No, he's not, actually. Where are you calling from?"

"Alberta. Zane's not answering my e-mails. Is your server down or something?"

"Um...no."

"Is he all right?"

"Yeah. He's fine. Look, Zanna, I like you and well...Zane's a moron. I have to tell you...he's seeing someone else."

An unexpected punch to the stomach. I can't breathe for a minute.

Mom was right. How can he let her be right? How could he be the cause of so many fights and then just give up on us because it's inconvenient?

"Zanna, are you there?"

"Yes. Could you tell him for me that we found Martin? He needs surgery on his leg but he's alive. We thought maybe he'd drowned."

"Geez, that's awful. I'm sorry." She waits a minute and I hear a big breath. "Zanna, I'm sorry about Zane too. His new girlfriend's a dork—nothing like you."

Why couldn't he have e-mailed me? Why did he let me go on making an idiot of myself? My face feels like it's on fire. I will it to cool down. "Listen, Imelda. Don't worry about it. We broke up before I left, anyway. We were just going to stay friends." A big lie that Zane could contradict if he wanted to. Still, right now, it makes me feel better. It's what Mom had advised me to do when she drove me over to Zane's that last time to say good-bye.

Tyler walks in as I put the receiver down. His lips lift into an almost-smile, but then he sees my face. "What's wrong? Is Martin okay?"

"My mother was right."

"That was her on the line?"

"No.... It was a friend. Never mind." I try to shake

the feeling away. "We came by because...I wanted to ask you..."

He steps closer. "Sure."

"Whether you'd look after Paris while we're at the hospital. In case we end up staying overnight and all..."

"Yes. I said yes, didn't I?" His words come out tense and clipped.

"Actually, you said 'sure' when you didn't know what I was asking."

Tyler shuts his eyes for a second and then looks to the side at his dad. He grabs my hands and tugs me away from the office area, away from Mr. Benson and Dad.

"Zanna," he whispers, "I would say yes to anything you ask me." His eyes stare into mine, the color of the lake in front of the cabin. "Tell me you weren't on the phone with your Toronto boyfriend." My face still feels hot; it's a dead giveaway.

"Technically I wasn't on the line with Zane so much as his sister."

Tyler drops my hands. "Come here, Paris. Come here, boy." He snaps his fingers. He's calling the dog but dismissing me. He's disappointed.

And he has a right to be. Haven't I been kissing Tyler? Shouldn't that have meant it was over between Zane and me? And at what moment precisely did it end? Was it with that first brush of Tyler's fingers against my ankle or with that last phone call? I'm confused too. I'll allow myself time later to think about that. No time right now, no chance to smooth anything over; we're in a hurry, anxious to be by Martin's bed when he wakes up. Anxious to get news. I don't allow myself to be anxious about one more thing, or person.

Dad paces in the hall outside the waiting room. I hump-swing a lot slower, back and forth. Every minute slows down into an hour. My left ankle pulses with pain and I'm almost sure I can feel the scalpel as it cuts into my brother. Finally at about three in the afternoon, the doctor calls out Dad's name. He's smiling. It must be good news.

He explains to us how badly Martin's leg is broken and how he needed to insert pins. There will need to be another surgery to remove them later.

"But that means he still has a leg, right?"

"Two, same as before."

"Woo-hoo!" I cheer and high-five Dad.

"He's still groggy but you can go in and see him now. Room 213." He points down the hall and Dad picks me and my crutches up so that he can run.

I push the door open and he puts me down inside the room. Martin looks so small and far away,
swallowed in white sheets and bandages. His right
leg hangs, white and huge from a pulley.

I hobble to his side, my left leg still bandaged. I
reach to hug him but stop, worrying that I will hurt
him.

"Like old times." He points to my ankle. "I wreck
my right side, you do the left."

The skinned knees, our broken arms: he remembers too. I smile.

"Want to be the first to sign?" he asks, pointing
to his cast.

"I didn't bring a pen, but sure. Let me see if someone can lend me something." In the lounge next
door, kids are watching TV and doing crafts. I saw
them during my many pacings down that hall. I end
up borrowing a whole set of markers.

When I return to Martin's side, he's in the middle
of a story. I don't interrupt, even though I instantly
know that I'm not just going to sign my name.

Instead I begin to draw. First, the donkey-like
ears...

"By the time I finally got the engine going again,
the fog had rolled in. I thought I could follow the trail
home, but one of the tires slipped off. I panicked and
gunned it. What a mistake! The ATV just flew."

I shade in the black and brown markings.

"In that mist I could barely make out the water, but I jumped anyway. Figured it would be the softest landing. But I hit a lot of rocks—man that hurt—and I passed out."

With a white marker, I draw the top of the heart around where his eyes would be.

"I think I would have drowned, but the water woke me up. I had to undo my shoe to get my foot loose from a rock."

Then I sketch in his strange yellow eyes. I work on them for a while, putting in the black pupils, trying to capture the fierceness, the loyalty.

"The current pulled me a long way away from the ATV and when I finally climbed out, I think I passed out again. Paris woke me—Paris and a couple of bears."

I finish drawing and look up at my brother.

"Paris scared the bears away, and then together we tried to make it home. I couldn't go on and Paris helped me, nudged me, actually, toward that cave you found me in. I was so cold, but I held on to him for warmth."

Dad interrupts. "Zanna, that's an incredible likeness. Martin, look what your sister drew on your cast."

Martin twists his head around. "Zanna. Wow.

You've got him down just perfect. You're just like Mom."

"No, I'm not," I snap.

"Okay. You're not talented," Martin coughs, "or beautiful." He mumbles the last words.

He's right, of course—Mom is all of those things. But she abandoned her family. I look at Dad and Martin and the picture of Paris. I'm never going to abandon them, ever. Or am I? I think ahead to September and feel my throat swell.

I wish I wasn't like my mother. I wish I didn't want to just drop everything and head for Paris too.

"Dad, do you think you could get me a Coke? I'm really thirsty," Martin says suddenly.

"Sure." Dad gets up and leaves Martin and me alone together.

I smile. My throat tightened. Martin needed a drink. Like old times.

"Zanna, Dad's working for Skylon," Martin tells me.

"Come on, Martin. How could you possibly know that for sure?"

"On his way out to Ribbon Glacier, he stopped to pick up a couple of guys with the Skylon emblem on their jackets."

"Okay, I can see why that makes it look like Dad's working with them, but you know him better than I do. Is there any way you could see Dad ever doing anything that could be bad for Ribbon Glacier? Or any glacier, for that matter?"

Martin shakes his head. "Or the polar ice caps, or any ice. Probably won't even put any in our drinks."

Sleepy and in pain as Martin must be, he smiles his big glow-ball smile. "You know, Mom's different but she's not as bad as you think, either." I won't agree with him, and he stays quiet for a moment. "It's going to be hard for me when you go back to her in September."

"That seems impossibly far away right now," I answer. It just seems impossible, really.

Dad returns with two Cokes, in cans, so no ice was sacrificed for our beverages. I gulp down half the drink immediately. I look at Dad and then Martin and want to hug them both. So I get up and start with Dad.

"Hey, what's this for?" my father says.

"I'm so glad to be living with you." Then it's Martin's turn, gently, gently. I want to fold the two of them up and tuck them into my heart, where I can carry them everywhere. They're really there already.

"Don't spill my drink!" Martin says as he frees himself. "Hey Dad, this picture of Paris," he points to his cast, "do you think we can save it somehow when the cast comes off?"

"You know what, Martin?" I say.

"What?"

"Don't worry about the picture on your cast. That's just a quick sketch. First piece of canvas I get, I'm going to do a full oil painting of your hero. Something you can have and keep forever." I stand up then. "Dad, can you lend me your credit card? I need to make a call to the Park Office, let them all know how Martin is."

And first chance I get to speak to Tyler, I'm going to try to make him understand how I feel about him. How it's him, not Zane, that I care about; how from the moment Tyler told me and Paris we had to leave the office, I fell for him. I just didn't know it until now. And if I can't do that on the phone immediately, I'll keep trying every day that I live in Last Chance Pass.

THE END